BOTS
HAZARDOUS MOTION

Nicole M. Taylor

EPIC
Press

Hazardous Motion
Bots: Book #2

Written by Nicole M. Taylor

Copyright © 2016 by Abdo Consulting Group, Inc.

Published by EPIC Press™
PO Box 398166
Minneapolis, MN 55439

Cover design by Dorothy Toth
Images for cover art obtained from iStockPhoto.com
Edited by Jennifer Skogen

Library of Congress Cataloging-in-Publication Data

Taylor, Nicole M.
Hazardous motion / Nicole M. Taylor.
p. cm. — (Bots ; #2)
Summary: No place is safe for Edmond West and his humanoid robot, Hart as they
are pursued not just by the US military, but also by the giant SennTech Corporation.
Meanwhile, the mass produced Bots are starting to think for themselves and they
don't think much of the jobs they've been asked to do.
ISBN 978-1-68076-002-6 (hardcover)
1. Robots—Fiction. 2. Robotics—Fiction. 3. Young adult fiction. I. Title.
[Fic]—dc23
2015932712

"Hazardous Motion": *Def. Unintended—and unexpected—motion from a robot that may cause injury.*

ONE

BLOODLINE

RIMMER RIVER, CALIFORNIA. SUMMER 2043

There was something visibly wrong with Hart's shoulder. Edmond suspected it was dislocated, though he couldn't say for sure with just a visual inspection. The shoulder was a relatively minor issue, however. The bigger problem by far was the wound at her throat, which had been a geyser of red and was now just a little anemic trickle.

In one important way, Hart's cardiovascular system worked much the same as a human's: it was essentially powered by hydraulics. If she lost too much blood and her blood pressure dipped too low, her heart wouldn't have the volume of liquid necessary to keep pumping. Eventually, she would power down. And Edmond didn't know if he could re-activate her here in the middle of nowhere in a no-tell motel with nothing in the way of equipment or tools.

So he would have to make sure that didn't happen.

The first problem he would have to solve was one of replacement. Hart had left quarts of her precious, finite blood supply on the floor of Edmond's car, soaked into the bed's sheets, splashed across pavement outside and the carpeted motel floor. He had no idea where to get more of it. Or even something sufficiently like it to fool Hart's sophisticated system.

Edmond had pulled her from the car and carried her into the room, using one hand to staunch the gush of blood from her wound. There was a man smoking in front of the front office who probably saw the whole clumsy affair but Edmond knew from the casual way he blew silvery smoke into the night air that he wouldn't say anything.

Edmond put Hart into the little bathtub with a compression bandage wrapped so tightly around her throat that she couldn't turn her head. Her eyelids had drooped steadily downwards until her eyes were just the faintest flickers of white sclera. It was an unconsciousness far deeper and more perilous than any of her little experimentations with human sleep.

The old saying was true, blood was considerably thicker than water, depending on a number of factors. Edmond ran the water in the sink to wash Hart's wasted blood off his hands and racked his brain. Motor oil? The idea had a certain ironic poetry to it, but he ultimately decided that wouldn't work either, as motor oil lacked the chemical structure that Hart required.

If he could just get access to a hospital, to a blood bank, anything. He had stopped at a drive through pharmacy to get the compression bandages and a packet of large-bore needles as well as a considerable length of hollow plastic tubing. He had also gotten some over the counter pain killers, though he had no idea how they might act on Hart's body. The pharmacy, not surprisingly, did not sell individual-use sacks of blood.

At the lab and afterwards, Hart had displayed a pain tolerance far beyond what Edmond would have thought possible. In theory, the gunshot should have sent her into shock immediately. Instead, she had remained more or less lucid until the blood loss got to her.

Edmond looked desperately around the little bathroom. A minuscule bottle of complimentary body wash. Opaque white conditioner. Nothing that could save her.

The only thing in that bathroom that bore any resemblance to blood was . . . blood. Edmond's blood, specifically. He turned his hands over, palms up and stretched out in front of him so he could see the criss-crossing blue spiderweb of his veins underneath his skin. It was the only viable solution. Perhaps it always had been.

It wasn't that he was squeamish, or at least not *just* that he was squeamish. Edmond had little in the way of medical training and performing an amateur blood-transfusion with himself as a donor in a dirty motel bathroom sounded like a good way to bleed to death or develop sepsis.

Despite his best efforts, Hart's blood had started to show through the compression bandage. Right now, the red stain was small. It looked like a tiny rosebud, just barely unfurled into life. He unspooled more of the gauze, wrapping it around and around her neck. Her head just flopped, weak and useless in his hands.

"Shit," Edmond said, reaching for the cardboard box full of latex gloves, purchased at that same drive-thru pharmacy. He had been worried that the checkout girl would be alarmed by his ominous collection of purchases, but she couldn't have been more uninterested as she passed the items out the window to him.

"Have an awesome night," she had said, not even looking directly at him.

Not exactly, Edmond thought as he pulled the syringe out of its packaging. For a moment, he was rendered immobile. *Left or right?* He was left-handed, so he should probably leave that one free to manipulate the tubing . . .

No. He had to attend to Hart first, before he gave up the use of one arm. Obviously. Edmond tried to remember how long it had been since he slept for any period of time. More than a day, at least. He was starting to get scattered and forgetful. He had to slow down, do things methodically. Both of them were depending on him not making a single mistake now.

First he had to find something to tie off their arms, raise the veins so the needles could find them more easily. After a quick search of the room, he grabbed the sash fastener on the curtains at the front of the room.

He tied one around Hart's upper arm, pulling it as tight as he dared. Her face didn't move, so he supposed she wasn't in pain. Her greenish veins popped into life in the soft hollow of her elbow and Edmond felt a long, rattling sigh escape from him, a breath he hadn't realized he was holding.

Still, it took him three tries to actually insert the needle into the vein.

"Sorry," he whispered, though she was surely unable to hear him.

Once the needle was in, he arranged her arm so it would lie as flat as possible and, hopefully, the needle wouldn't move around or—worst of all— slip out entirely. *Tape*, he berated himself, *I should have bought tape.*

Edmond's hand was shaking as he awkwardly looped the curtain tie around his own forearm. If he remembered his (minimal) medical training, he needed to connect to an artery and there was a good one at the base of the wrist. The material was thick and ribbed like corduroy. He used his teeth to hold one end while he pulled the other tight. He tried not to think about where this particular piece of fabric had been.

Oddly enough, it was easier getting the second needle into his own arm. Possibly because he had already practiced on poor Hart. He watched as his blood spilled red and robust into the hollow tube.

Edmond closed his eyes for a moment. He had that feeling that he had always gotten on those occasions when he'd donated blood, as though the room were ever so slightly tilted around him. It was like the onset of drunkenness and he had to close his eyes and forget about the warm sensation of his own blood, outside his body, dripping along a thin plastic tube.

He sat down on the toilet, bracing himself with his left hand and flexing and unflexing his right. Slowly, the clear plastic tube turned red. He watched as his blood made its way into Hart's body.

Edmond swallowed hard, his throat had suddenly grown soft and dry as a cotton ball. He leaned his head back against the bathroom wall. It was pleasantly cool against his head which, he realized now, was slick with sweat.

When did I start sweating? he wondered. It was the last coherent thought he had.

---◯---

Upon waking, Edmond thought, for just the briefest instant, that everything was okay. He was back in his bed in his little apartment. He was probably late for work but ten years of late nights and early mornings should buy him some latitude . . .

But his bed wasn't this hard. His blankets did not have this abrasive, carnival-plastic texture. His room did not smell like mildew and cheap hand soap. This was not his home and he would never go back to the lab again. He sat up suddenly and, just as suddenly, went back down, his vision almost immediately going black. His limbs were shockingly weak; if he had been standing, he would have fallen over.

Edmond laid flat for a few moments and breathed deep. He sat up again, but slowly this time. His vision telescoped slightly and he stretched out his hand to prop himself up. There was a bandage around his wrist. A cluster of cotton balls crisscrossed with two novelty band-aids made to look like strips of bacon. He had definitely not purchased those. Someone had also wrapped an ace bandage around his wrist to support the entire construction.

Someone had drawn the curtains closed, though there were slashes of bright sunshine along the bottom. He must have slept through most of the day. On top of the television, there was a small carton of chocolate milk, like he'd gotten with his lunches in grade school. There was also a box of swiss rolls and a large bag of cheese puffs.

Hart. Hart must have done all this for him.

The thought triggered some old sensation, a

familiarity that he struggled to place. It was old, from before his father had left, even. A memory. The family had gone on some sort of long car trip, Edmond didn't remember any trip or what they might have seen there. But he remembered unclipping his seat belt and stretching out along the length of the backseat. He had made a patchwork blanket out of his parents' discarded coats.

He remembered bumping along their dirt road and slowing as they approached the trailer. Edmond had squeezed his eyes shut and laid as still as possible. He breathed slowly and shallowly, air tumbling out of his mouth rather than being forcibly propelled. He allowed his forehead to wrinkle ever so slightly when the car doors opened and the interior dome light cast a yellow glow on his face.

He must have known then that this time in his life was soon drawing to a close, or else he would not have bothered pretending to sleep, in the hopes that his father would pick him up and carry him into the house. Already, he must have been conscious of how he was growing and how the world was changing. Perhaps even conscious of the omnipresent tension between his parents.

His father did indeed pick him up, Edmond remembered that. His chest was warm, though his bare forearms were cold. He smelled like cigarettes and a little bit like engine grease. Pressed against his chest, Edmond could hear the slow, regular throb of his heart and, when he laid Edmond down in his bed, it felt like the softest, most luxurious resting place imaginable.

It was better for his consciousness of it. Edmond didn't know if that was the last time they had carried him into the house, but it was the last time that he remembered being . . . cradled, in that fashion. As though he were no burden at all, at least no burden that anyone might struggle with.

Hart must have done something like that. For someone who could run through solid metal doors, carrying Edmond would be like carrying the lightest of children. Edmond searched his memory for some idea, some scrap of sensation, but there was nothing but darkness in his mind.

His vision mostly clear, Edmond swung his feet over the edge of the bed and stood up. He could still feel a certain trembling weariness in his limbs, as though his body were a huge, fleshy vehicle that he was controlling inexpertly. He leaned on the walls as he made his way towards the little bathroom.

The door was cracked slightly and light poured out. Inside, someone was running the tap. Edmond knocked on the door with two fingers. He stumbled backwards as the door swung out towards him, Hart's anxious face appearing like a magic trick. She held a washcloth in one hand, it was orange-y pink with her blood.

One side of her throat was an ugly, meandering embroidery, bright blue stitches stark against her skin. She was clearly no great seamstress, but she had closed up the hole in her neck and the blood that was there appeared crusted and dry.

She smiled at him, so soft and, for the first time, sad.

"Thank you," she said.

"What happened?" Edmond asked, his voice creaking unexpectedly.

"I woke up," Hart said, as though that explained it all. She turned back to the mirror, wiping delicately at her neck, careful not to disturb her stitches. On the sink, Edmond spotted a small portable sewing kit, of the sort used to restore lost buttons. A needle, threaded through with blue floss, lay on the sink. The needle's tip was red and the slightly damp place where it lay was a delicate pink color.

"You fixed yourself," Edmond said stupidly. Hart nodded.

"I had a small nick in my external carotid. I closed it up. It will heal now."

When she said "small nick," Edmond immediately became conscious of a similar pain in his wrist. He extended it towards her. "Did you do this, too?"

Hart reached out to touch the bandage in a fond way, the way someone might handle an old and fragile picture from childhood. "I saw those at the store. They were the most expensive, so I thought they would be the best. Does it hurt?"

Her fingertips on his skin were still so soft. Softer, it seemed, than human skin could be. Edmond shook his head, rendered momentarily mute.

Hart opened up her own elbow, showed him the bandages on her arm. "We match now," she said.

She had her color back, her cheeks and her throat were a coral shade. The blood was pumping into her veins and capillaries, swelling and contracting according to the temperature, her physical condition, her emotions. Edmond imagined his blood swimming in hers, complementary but distinct. Or would his blood simply disappear into hers and become indistinguishable?

"Cheesy puffs," he found himself saying.

"I wasn't sure what to buy," Hart admitted. "The boy at the register said they were his favorite."

"And the chocolate milk?"

"That too."

Edmond almost chuckled. He'd gotten the stoner prix fixe menu.

Her shirt was stiff and raised, dried blood holding it in position against her skin. Edmond wondered if she had gone out looking like that, like someone who had just gotten shot in the throat. He wondered if anyone noticed and if they had cared. "If you're okay, we should go."

"Where are we going?" Hart asked him. It was a question Edmond had devoted considerable thought to. In the days before they fled the lab, he had actually purchased a burner pre-paid cell phone and called his mother late one night, asking for her advice. They couldn't leave the country, at least not via the usual channels—Hart didn't even have a passport and Edmond's was surely flagged. Edmond had little family, fewer friends; there was no one, in fact, besides his mother who might be persuaded to help him at great risk to their personal safety.

His mother had sighed into the phone. It seemed that, somehow, she had seen this, or something like it, coming. "I don't know if you remember but, when you were about two, your Dad went away for a little while."

"I don't really remember that, no," Edmond said. His father "went away" pretty regularly, he hardly recalled each specific instance.

"No, I mean he went to prison. For eighteen months. It was a DUI thing. You never asked about it, so I didn't say anything. But he met these guys while he was there, they were in for some sort of minor drug bust, but they were actually working an illegal grow operation up in Oregon."

"They all got out around the same time and your Dad did some work for them. He lived up there for a couple of months, doing security. If they're still there, they might help you. At the very least, they won't ask a lot of questions. Maybe they could even help you with documents and things like that."

It was a straw and a spindly one at that, but Edmond had grasped it nonetheless.

"We're almost there," he told Hart. She nodded, processing this information.

"Then why did we stop?"

Beside them, the bathtub was still streaked a startling rusty orange with her blood. "For you," Edmond said. "Of course."

Hart turned back to the sink and collected her little makeshift sewing kit. She tossed a fistful of bandage wrappers into the trash and swept the remains up into a plastic bag from a convenience store.

"I want you to teach me to drive today," she said, sealing up the bag with two fingers. Something had changed in her since she'd awoken. But then, maybe it had been longer than that. There was something brittle and skittish about her now, a little tarnish to her shine. Her mouth turned down more than he remembered.

"Sure," he said. "How are you feeling?"

The question appeared to take Hart by surprise. She held the plastic bag in both hands, holding it over her stomach like a shield between the two of them. She was silent for a long moment, she appeared to be giving the question a level of consideration that Edmond hadn't really expected.

Finally, she spoke: "I will be better soon."

TWO

FRIENDLY FIRE

DISPUTED TERRITORY, FORMER POLAND. JANUARY, 2045

The woman—she had identified herself only as "Kinga"—was younger than she looked, Hart Series C-27699 knew that. War had a way of putting years on someone. A face that had been plump starved out into something sagging and miserable, soft skin draping like premature wrinkles. A knit hat covered most of her head, but wisps of hair so light it might have been blonde or silver escaped on all sides. Her eyes were clear and bright, however, a watery blueish-grey. She looked at C-27699 frankly and expectantly. He looked back.

"Dzień dobry—"

"I speak English," the woman snapped. She did

and with a minimal, geographically ambiguous accent. Hart Series C-27699 wondered what she had done before the war. Usually, C-27699 did not have to inquire about such things. Most people loved to talk about what their lives used to be like. "Before the war, I was . . . " "Before the war, I did . . . "

Kinga did not offer any additional biographical details, however.

The woman rubbed her hands together, angry scarlet with chilblains. They were meeting in what had been, until forty-six hours previously, a hotel. Now, the dizzying penthouses had been sheared off on one side, leaving the building lop-sided and open to the sky. Metal struts poked out into the air and the glass doors at the entrance were still standing, though crazed with cracks. Bizarrely, one entire conference room was more or less intact and the two of them occupied an absurdly large wooden table.

It wasn't unaffected however. A bomb had

ripped a good-sized hole in the roof and it was bitterly cold outside. It was starting to snow and, periodically, a single hardy snowflake would make it all the way down to the table and land on one of them.

Hart Series C-27699 had been told that the site had been vetted and would be safe, but, looking up into the passing clouds made him wonder how true that was.

"Can we hurry?" the woman pressed and the Hart Series wondered if she was concerned about additional bombings or if she were simply very cold. When Hart Series C-27699 was assigned to the Russian conflict zones, he was updated with cold-weather resistant add-ons. He still wore a thick anorak and gloves, however, for the look if nothing else.

"Certainly," he said to her "Look, my superiors are a little concerned by some of the recent operations. They have an . . . " he paused. Her hard eyes bored into his. " . . . anti-American tang."

She snorted. It was loud and somehow obscene. It seemed to echo a little bit against the incomplete walls. Hart Series C-27699 had been somewhat prepared for this sort of reaction. The president's comments on television about the homegrown Western Slav resistance surely had not improved the feeling on the ground. There was even some talk of committing troops to the Russian coalition's efforts in the disputed territory of Former Ukraine, which was bound to make C-27699's job a lot more interesting.

"You're not the only game in town," the Hart Series cautioned. "We can take our offer elsewhere."

In truth, he expected to hold at least three more meetings identical to this one. There were the ethnic Poles, the various refugee groups and, of course, the Christian Martyr Movement. All his superiors really needed was a promise of good behavior, no matter how transparently false. *"Yes, sir, we'll be just as good as gold with the killing machines that you give us."*

"At this time, we have no intention to move against American targets," the woman said slowly, choosing each word with exquisite care.

"At this time?"

Kinga spread her hands wide as if indicating the entire broken hotel, the snow and the sky beyond it. "Who can promise the future?"

Part of the Hart Series' job on these specific missions was to see if he could determine whether or not his contacts were being truthful. He had found, however, that this typically worked much less well than his superiors had imagined. That was a general theme of his work, however. He could analyze the woman's diction pattern to determine how many unique words she used in conversation (a high incidence of repeat words was a good indicator of deception) though he suspected that people were getting wise to this tactic. Perhaps that was why this woman insisted on speaking in her second language.

He could observe their heart rate and respiration,

but that was a notoriously unreliable technique. And these types of encounters had a way of putting people on edge anyway. The simple fact was that human beings were very good at lying and even better at rationalizing their lies. Even their bodies obeyed.

So what would he write when it came time to report on this meeting? *"Leader of rebel faction seems no better or worse than any of the others. Should sow plenty of confusion. Violence will surely ensue."*

"I guess we have a deal, then," the Hart Series said, extending his hand.

The woman took it and held it a beat too long, looking thoughtful as though the texture of his skin was somehow puzzling to her.

"And you," she said, "where are you from?" It was the first time she had taken any interest in him as an individual. Hell, he still didn't know her real name, "Kinga" being an obvious code name. He must have looked puzzled, because she elaborated. "Your voice. You have a little bit of an accent."

That shouldn't be right. Hart Series C-27699 had been rigorously educated and great care had been taken to make him a perfect chameleon. In Dusseldorf, he was a German, in Monterey, a Mexican. He was not so much a blank slate as an empty frame, unexceptional in its own right but designed to highlight each unique work of art that fit into it.

"Lots of places," he said finally. "All over."

Kinga started to say something, but her words were consumed by a distant whine and a terrible thumping, like muffled thunder. Her eyes widened visibly. If he were monitoring her heart rate, he suspected it would spike wildly.

Immediately, she stood up and allowed her chair to fall to the floor, crouching down to scramble underneath the table. HS C-27699 followed her lead; he knew very well what that sound was. He had been specifically told that this meeting was being conducted in a "safe" zone where he could expect to be free from bombardment. Apparently not.

If he were to ask his superiors, he was sure they would say something about unforeseen events and the inherently unpredictable nature of an active combat zone. Underneath the table, the two of them were utterly silent, as though drones could hear their chatter. HS C-27699 listened carefully, trying to determine just from the sound what kind of explosion he was hearing.

Judging by the sound, the explosion was still fairly far away. If it was a homemade explosive planted by an opposing guerrilla force or even just a particularly violent street gang, they were likely far from the blast range and almost certainly not the intended target. If it was any one of a number of groups that had access to American firepower . . .

HS C-27699 did not have a god and was only dimly aware of the function of such constructions, but he knew that, in these types of situations, people typically asked for God's assistance.

He realized that, beside him, Kinga was shaking violently. She had her hands tucked up underneath her arms, holding her ribcage so hard that her teeth were grinding audibly from the effort. For a moment, C-27699 thought that she was afraid but, looking at her face, he saw more anger than anything else.

Her shivers were involuntary, her body produced them at the sound of bombs and there was nothing she could do to stop them. It was as though the fear had infected her flesh but not her mind. It took any way out that it could find.

HS C-27699 did not have such a fear response. He imagined that even were he to experience many, many bombings, he would never quake like that. His body would not store up the fear and be overcome by it, it could not. That was a massive design flaw and his creators surely would have elided such obviously unhelpful features.

There was a long, low whistle, like someone summoning a dog, and another thudding sound, closer now. Multiple bombings approaching their location. C-27699 registered this information but wasn't sure exactly what to do with it. He could not call in his position in hope of rescue. His superiors would probably rather not know where he was, all things considered. He wondered idly if he had brokered a deal to provide the munitions that were now raining down on him.

Beside him, Kinga was looking down at her knees. Still shaking. It looked almost painful, like an epileptic's spasms. C-27699 thought about comforting her in some way, perhaps reaching out to place a hand on her shoulder. He did not think such a gesture would be welcome coming from him, however.

A third blast, this one much closer. So close, in fact, that some dusty fragments shook free from the ruined ceiling above them. HS C-27699 watched them rain down on either side of the table. It occurred to him that the table was not actually protective in any but the most cursory way.

He tilted his head up to examine the underside of the table. It was fairly thick, made of redwood or something similar. C-27699 figured it would deflect pieces of debris weighing anything from one-half to six pounds. If what remained of the ceiling fell in, however, the table would almost certainly be crushed and them beneath it.

HS C-27699 wondered what happened to a Bot who was destroyed in the field. He did not suppose anyone would recover his remains. He had been made explicitly aware that, should he be captured or confined while in the field, the US military would make no efforts whatsoever to extract him. If they wouldn't come fetch his functioning body he couldn't imagine they would dispatch someone to sift through a debris field looking for pieces of him.

Technically, none of the Hart Series Bots were classified as soldiers or even as assets. They were, C-27699 remembered, Military Equipment (Other).

The fourth explosion was so close that the floor underneath shook. C-27699 had never experienced an earthquake. He supposed this was as close as he was going to get.

Even if he had wanted to, even if he thought it would do some good, HS C-27699 could not contact any of his handlers. Two days ago, he had been pickpocketed by a group of children, none of them older than fourteen, and they had taken his flex-tablet as well as the scant amount of American money he had on him. C-27699 was not particularly worried about the tablet—he had his instructions for the near future, including this meeting with Kinga and his superiors would quickly notice irregular activity on the device. It was hardly the first time a soldier had lost a flex-tablet in the field, but it might have been the most ridiculous.

It was an absurdly transparent trick, a kitten who needed coaxing out of a pile of rubble. The kitten was afraid and had made a kind of den amongst the broken bits of wood and crumbled masonry, but the children were worried, they said, that the whole thing was going to collapse and kill the cat.

HS C-27699 had crouched patiently in front of the rubble. He could just make out the kitten's eyes, that astonishing, watery blue of the newly-born. He stretched out his hands and was exceptionally still, waiting for the cat to trust him. He never even felt them lift his rucksack and ferret out his flex-tablet.

After more than fifteen minutes of perfect stillness, the kitten cautiously emerged. It kept ducking its head, as though it were avoiding the light. It tottered towards his fingers and gave them a supremely skeptical sniff. Outside of its hovel, it was a very pretty little thing. Mostly the color of smoke with a tiny white face.

When it drew close enough, C-27699 closed his hands around it so fast that two of the children jolted. The kitten panicked for a second, scrabbling its needle claws against his knuckles. He held it gently but firmly and, eventually, the cat relaxed, apparently realizing that its wild wriggling was accomplishing nothing at all.

He gave the cat to a little girl of eight or nine. She thanked him so sincerely that he should have known right then what they had been up to. As it was, he didn't even discover the flex-tablet was missing until the next morning.

In some ways, it had been a relief. He had come to regard the flex-tablet as disproportionately heavy. He was always acutely aware of it, always thinking about how he should be preparing intelligence reports and getting new assignments. He had taken to keeping it in his rucksack all the time so he never had to look at it. When he realized it was, in fact, missing, there was a little swell of giddiness in his chest.

Now, though, his only lifeline, and a meager one at that, was gone and its absence seemed particularly acute. For a few days at least, C-27699 would be alone.

Kinga was breathing shallowly through her mouth.

The Hart Series didn't know whether this was a calming mechanism or just an escalation of her physiological fear response. Her people would come to find her, he realized. They would search the rubble for days, if that was what it took. They would bury her according to her customs and near the people she had loved.

C-27699 didn't know who she had been before the war, but she knew and her people knew. They would honor her in death and show their gratitude for her sacrifice.

By his count, it had been nine minutes since the last bomb. The previous explosions had been less than five minutes apart. Perhaps the action was complete now? The woman did not move, but remained in a low crouch, staring at her own knees, her mouth open and her breath just skimming her lips.

C-27699 moved decisively, though in no particular direction. He scrambled out from underneath the table and stood up. Kinga would probably be stiff after all that sustained crouching. Hart Series C-27699 was not stiff. Hart Series C-27699 was in full working order.

He reached out a hand to help Kinga to her feet. Her eyebrows knit together when she looked at him. She was incredulous. "No," she said, as though he were very stupid. "They may not be done."

"No," C-27699 agreed, "they may not."

He left the remains of the old hotel through the proper door and not the one a bomb had made.

They called it, somewhat sarcastically, the Hotel American. It wasn't actually a hotel and it was neither run by nor exclusively for Americans. In reality, it was probably part of a college campus or perhaps some kind of secondary school. The accommodations were obviously retrofitted dorm rooms with two or four beds in each suite.

It was sparsely populated nearly all the time, so C-27699 had never actually needed to share a room, which he appreciated. The beds were not particularly comfortable or uncomfortable and the noise was perpetual, but the hotel sat on the Czech side of the border and was thus, more or less, secure. All of the intelligence that Hart Series C-27699 had been privy to indicated that the Czech Republic was considered a "low-profile target" for re-absorption into the Russian Empire. It would be months, if not years, before the situation became perilous.

At the moment, he was sharing space with a large group of private contractors. He rarely saw them as their schedules did not exactly mesh. He experienced them mainly as a cacophony of boots in the hallway.

They must be gone now, because all he heard was silence. Out the window, it was still snowing but weakly in little spurts.

By the time he arrived at the hotel, a package

had arrived for him. It was a sleek tube, fastened at both ends with a clever iris-scanner to prevent mail tampering. It was almost certainly a replacement flex-tablet, which made sense. C-27699 had a debriefing scheduled for the next morning, and his superiors would be very interested in his meeting with Kinga and her counterparts amongst the other various groups.

He did not open the package.

Instead, he was thinking about that smoke-gray kitten and the children. He was thinking about how that was the first assignment he had ever felt good about completing. In fact, it was one of the few assignments he could even say he had completed. Most of the time, HS C-27699 did as he was ordered and then moved on to the next task, never finding what, if anything, he had done.

It was absurd. Luring a kitten from a pile of rubble. A trick designed to distract him while he was robbed, it would be ridiculous to feel a sense of accomplishment about that. And yet, he did. He basked in it.

As he walked back from his meeting with Kinga, he had peered into buildings and doorways at the shapes huddled there. Some of them shook like Kinga and some others stretched their bodies over their friends, lovers, comrades in arms. There were places where teams of people had obviously fortified a single building against street-level fire and other structures where men and women with weapons stood guard outside.

He was the only person on the street. The snow collected in his hair. He could feel all their eyes upon him as he walked.

If he had died right then, if the bombs had fallen on his head, he might have been obliterated and no one would ever have known. The military would not investigate his death, none of his contacts on the ground expected to see him more than once.

When a kitten got trapped in a pile of wood and stone, there were half a dozen children willing to rescue it. It was so easy for a Hart Series to become a ghost. Just about the easiest thing in the world.

The snow had melted into his hair and dampened it into a shiny seal-black. He laid on his little cot-bed, soaking the lumpy pillow with cold water.

"Where are you from?" Kinga had asked him and he had told her everywhere.

But now, he was realizing, everywhere was just another way of saying nowhere.

THREE

BOOM

SAN DOMENICA, CALIFORNIA. JANUARY, 2045.

"Another one?"

Janelle knew that Liao was upset because he had bothered to make the journey all the way down to the lab. Of course, she had a pretty good idea about what had gotten stuck in his craw.

"That's fourteen," he said, waving an actual paper printout of the e-memo in one hand. If Janelle was braver, she would have reported to him personally. She was trying to avoid this exact conversation, but she should have known better. General Liao had been breathing down her neck since the first Hart Series robot defected and the rapid uptick in such cases wasn't doing anything to improve his mood.

"Yes," Janelle said, "I know." She was particularly disappointed in HS C-27699. She had always been fond of him, perhaps because she had modeled him on her first great love, Alex Portillo. She gave him the same sleek black hair and unusually large, expressive green eyes, the broad, ready smile that had endeared him to so many of her contemporaries. She recognized, of course, what a potential breech of professionalism that was, so she had always taken care to keep HS C-27699 at a distance. She was not his primary caregiver, she did not provide any of his education, she rarely saw him, in fact. But when she did, she could not help but think of Alex Portillo and the summer after her fourteenth birthday when she'd first gotten her braces off.

"I have the whole team working right now to find an appropriate solution to the problem," Janelle reassured him.

Liao frowned. "I don't want an appropriate solution. I want a fast and effective solution."

Arguably the same thing, Janelle thought but did not say.

"You do realize that HS Bots now have a higher incidence of AWOL than actual human soldiers?" Liao continued.

"Yes, we think it has something to do with the way Bots are deployed. They are not developing those intense interpersonal bonds that soldiers in traditional units have." Janelle could see, even as she was explaining, that Liao was preparing to shut her down.

It wasn't that Janelle did not like her new position as Lead Roboticist of the program. In many ways, nothing about her responsibilities and expectations had changed. After all, Edmond had been the nominal head of the department but virtually all of the administrative tasks had always been left up to Janelle. She had always done the wrangling for more funding, more interns, more equipment, and, more often than not, she had borne the brunt of any official disproval. Early in his military career it became clear that criticism and even rage utterly failed to penetrate Edmond West's surprisingly thick skin.

It was somehow different now that it had been codified and made official.

Janelle didn't want to think of herself as having been . . . bolstered in some way by Edmond, but she did have to admit that it had been easier when she had someone else to bounce ideas off of, even if his responses were frequently unhelpful if not non-existent.

For years, she had labored in her field waiting for the day that someone would finally acknowledge her skill and her hard work. Instead, she had watched a succession of Bright Young Men like Edmond—and they were young men, usually young, *white* men as well—meet and surpass her with nothing more than their boundless "potential."

Her proven track record of excellence meant nothing next to what some upstart genius *might* one day accomplish.

And, like Edmond, almost all of them had flamed out in some spectacular fashion. Janelle felt that this tendency towards self-destruction had to be somehow tied to their above-average intelligence. Perhaps the traits that caused massive personal problems came bundled with those like superior reasoning skills? Or, even more likely, they were simply young people who had always been certain of being the smartest person in any given room. They were unused to being wrong and incapable of diagnosing the symptoms.

Janelle had tried to help Edmond, more than any of the others, even. But Edmond was so profoundly single-minded. It was probably what allowed him to develop the Hart Series in the first place, but it also gave him tunnel vision. Like the critiques of their superiors, Janelle's words of caution had slid off of him like eggs off a greased skillet.

She realized suddenly that Liao had been talking all the time that she had been musing.

"—not a therapy session," he was saying. "I just want them to follow orders."

For the first time, Janelle noticed a smudgy darkness under Liao's eyes. She realized that the uncertainties and pressures she faced in her new position must be magnified exponentially for someone in his. Plus there was the . . . issue of Edmond.

Edmond West had been Liao's pet. He brought the boy in and insisted on putting him in the program. He offered Edmond far more latitude than anyone else would have gotten. And now it had blown up in his face.

If not for the fact that they had recovered Edmond's notes and were able to replicate his research, Janelle was confident that General Liao's career would have evaporated along with Edmond and his prototype. But the Hart Series program was in no way a sure-fire success and each setback reflected unavoidably on Liao and, trickling down, on Janelle.

And, Janelle had to admit, this was not a small flaw. A propensity for ignoring orders and simply walking away from assignments in the field was about as disastrous as possible when it came to Problems You Could Have With Your Humanoid Robots. Liao's harangues had a great deal of truth in them: they needed to solve this problem quickly because all of their livelihoods were at stake.

"I want a progress report by the end of the week," Liao said. "And it should contain some actual progress." He frowned at her and Janelle nodded fervently back at him.

A week. If she had three to five years she could perform a series of controlled studies of the Bots both alone and amongst their peers. With that information, she could tweak their neural programming to ensure a more stable, cohesive personality for each individual Bot.

But Janelle did not have three to five years. She had one week.

In one week, there were only a handful of remotely efficacious solutions, the most obvious of which was the idea of a kill switch. Some sort of feature or element introduced into the Bots' physiology that could allow humans to remotely destroy a unit that was swerving off-message, becoming dangerous, or fleeing from an assignment.

If it had been up to her, she never would have put the Bots in the field so soon. They were barely tested and thus wholly unpredictable. But General Liao had to show the doubters that the program worked, that Edmond's research was viable and useful.

"Yes, sir," Janelle said finally. "I will have progress for you by the end of the week."

Edmond's place in the lab was now occupied, more or less, by three young interns. Hector Flores,

Kadence DeSouza, and Eun-hye Kim. Janelle had instituted a lab policy about not using Bots of any series as assistants in their work. The more issues that cropped up with Bot personality flaws, the more unsafe that practice seemed.

The interns were on board with the kill switch almost immediately. Hector quickly got to work on the methodology of the device. They needed something unobtrusive and as rapidly fatal as possible.

They also, of course, needed something that could be triggered remotely. A tertiary but not wholly irrelevant concern was the issue of pain and suffering. Janelle made it clear that the kill switch was not a torture device and should not be used in that capacity. Insofar as it was possible, they needed to avoid causing trauma to the Bots.

Eun-hye, whose formal training was in neurology, agreed to study the existing population of Bots in the lab with the hope of identifying the neurological components of undesirable behavior.

Kadence would work on the "remote control" aspect of the technology.

Though each one of them had very distinct personalities (awkward Hector, cutting Eun-hye, carefree Kadence) they all attacked the problem of the kill switch design with the same sense of curious enthusiasm. It was as though Janelle had asked them to prepare a science fair project, rather than develop a device for ending lives, synthetic though they may be.

It was in these moments that Janelle thought somewhat wistfully about Edmond. It was true that they had never gotten along perfectly and there had been much about him that frustrated her to no end. But they had worked together for nearly a decade, and one develops a certain rhythm over time, a simpatico that cannot be forced or conjured into being.

Janelle's grandmother, the woman who had raised her, said that she hadn't properly grieved for Edmond. The older woman had no idea what, specifically, had happened, but she did know that Janelle had lost a co-worker.

"Allow yourself to be sad," her grandmother advised. "Because it's going to come out, one way or another."

Janelle made it very clear that they were on a stringent deadline. She made certain that each of the interns was acutely aware of the end of the week and what it meant for all of them.

None of them were geniuses like Edmond. Thankfully. When she put them to work, they automatically stepped up production, working through the nights and subsisting on caffeine supplements and fifteen-minute naps in the medical rooms. They did not have supernatural intellect to back them up, so they were forced to simply work very, very hard.

And it paid off. Hector was first to bring her an actionable idea. He had based his kill switch around the very real behavior of a cerebral aneurysm. When it killed, it did so rapidly, leaving little time for the victim to suffer unduly. He suggested that they create a device that mimicked the look and function of a massive ruptured brain aneurysm.

Thus, when a Bot was demonstrating undesirable behavior, someone on the ground could trigger the mechanism and flood their brain with blood. The pressure would stop their brain function within a matter of moments.

He was very proud of his design, showing Janelle model after model on his flex tablet. It looked rather unassuming, a little pendular glob, purplish in color. He suggested that they implant it against the inside of every Bot's skull where it would linger, utterly harmless, until activated.

It was Eun-hye who suggested making all of the Bots aware of the kill switch. She had been concentrating most of her work on HS D-94128, a well-known "problem child" in the lab.

In fact, HS D-94128 had been in the lab longer than all of the other Bots (and some of the interns).

She had never been cleared for active duty, which wasn't a great surprise, all things considered.

Janelle knew that with a scaled-up Bot production, they were bound to come across more and more "bad eggs" amongst the reliable. There were now more than three hundred "completed" Bots scattered between the laboratory and the field and several had presented with what the lab was calling "compliance issues." Even amongst the troubled Bots, HS D-94128 was a special case and infinitely fascinating as far as the kill switch project was concerned.

D-94128 was constantly on lockdown for negative behavior. She refused to attend her designated appointments and had, on three occasions, attempted to leave the lab without an escort. Janelle wasn't sure one could call what she was doing an "escape attempt" as she seemed to have no cogent plan for what she would do when she got outside the base. Rather, D-94128 simply wanted to do things for the sake of doing them, or for the sake of self-determination.

She was determinedly antisocial and she had frequently become violent with the other Bots, once with a lab tech. Her enhanced strength made that propensity no small issue. After she ripped a fellow Bot's ear nearly off his head, she was put on a daily regimen of sedatives. It made her logy and ineffectual, if not actually tractable. It was the best way they had found of controlling her behavior.

Now, she was Eun-hye's guinea pig, spending most of her days with a series of neural monitors affixed to her head (most of the Bots chose to let their hair grow in after activation. HS D-94128 had thrown a fit when caretakers refused to keep shaving her head. She had somehow figured out how to vomit on cue and she did so until officials relented and started cutting her hair weekly. No one was dumb enough to give her a razor, even an electric one).

D-94128, startlingly, didn't seem to mind this

extended testing process. Or rather, she minded it less than anything else she might have been obliged to do with her time. She disliked education, or at least the type of education that the lab was providing her. She did not enjoy training, except for running. She could, if given the opportunity, run all day. She would run until her entire body collapsed.

Under Eun-hye's watchful eye she was allowed relatively unfettered Internet access, something the Bots almost never got in their usual day-to-day. Eun-hye reported that she mostly spent her time listening to music. She also like to watch videos with dogs in them. HS D-94128 seemed agnostic about animals in general, but something about dogs, specifically videos of them running and jumping, was very compelling for her.

This, of course, was a distinct part of Eun-hye's research. She wanted to monitor HS D-94128 through the widest possible array of emotions. To that end, she had even taken D-94128 outside to the little green area just behind the parking lot. Eun-hye had allowed her to move freely (or as freely as possible, given the constraints of her monitors) while Eun-hye followed patiently along behind her, recording every spike and blip inside her brain.

"Knowledge of the kill switch will prevent non-compliant behavior," Eun-hye said. "Simple self-preservation. We can also build in a kind of hierarchical warning system. I've been talking to Hector and he says that there is no reason we can't design the kill switch to ramp up in intensity. If we issue a kind of "pulse" at the first sign of resistance or rebellion, that will give the Bots a physical guideline for what is and is not appropriate."

She paused and offered a knowing smile.

"Of course, as my research has indicated, the Bots know very well when they are violating orders. The orbitofrontal area of HS D-94128's brain is highly active when she's doing things she knows to be in contradiction to a direct order."

"What about indirect orders?" Janelle asked.

After all, no one had explicitly told C-27699 not to run off through the wilds of Eastern Europe.

"The Bots are highly intelligent and they have a high level of reasoning ability. Because so many of the earlier iterations were such staunch literalists, the Hart Series is actually more capable of reading non-specific cues and acting accordingly. D-94128's brain shows similar activity when she does or says things that she merely thinks are likely prohibited."

"So we wouldn't even have to necessarily monitor their behavior," Janelle said, "just their neurological reaction to their behavior."

Eun-hye nodded. "It would be an even more pronounced reaction if we introduced the concept of the kill switch because then you're talking about a built-in apprehension and anxiety around those non-compliant choices. There will be immediate, obvious neurological changes whenever a Bot does something they know will activate their kill switch thus . . . activating their kill switch."

All of this actually gelled nicely with Kadence's work on remotely controlling the Bots. She had struggled with the idea of how to determine when the Bots were "going off the reservation" as she said, proposing a number of expensive and bulky solutions: biologically integrated cameras, satellite observation, buddy teams of Bots in the field. None of them seemed particularly viable to Janelle.

"Oh yeah," Kadence said when Eun-hye presented her findings, "that's a lot better. We already have a GPS unit free-floating in the Bot's bloodstream, it would be relatively easy to modify it to report on other stats. We could even look at heartbeat, respiration, all sorts of health data."

"The GPS," Janelle said, "has been circumvented." C-27699 and the others who had fled their assignments had somehow figured out how to find and deactivate—or possibly remove—the GPS trackers inside their bodies. The data consistently showed the Bots tracked as normal for a short period of time and then, abruptly, disappearing.

There was no commonality in the geographic locations or in the Bots themselves and no one in the lab had proposed an explanation for how this was being done. Or, more critically, a solution.

"But that's disobeying an order, right?" Kadence said. "An implicit order. But still. As soon as they try to dig that tracker out"—she placed her closed fist against the side of her head—"BOOM." She opened her hand like a star.

---O---

When it came to the idea of a test run, there was really only ever one likely candidate. HS D-94128 was a strange appendix upon the program. She wasn't in any way suited for normal Bot occupation and she was generally disruptive and difficult in the lab. She had a certain level of research value but it was infinitely more important that the kill-switch technology be tested on an actual Bot. The information they would glean from this experiment was vastly more useful than any function HS D-94128 might perform in the future.

D-94128 had appeared in enough incident reports that her designation was undoubtably familiar to the program's overseers. That was the only explanation Janelle could imagine for the incredibly quick turnaround on her "equipment management" request.

As for HS D-94128, she likely had a sense of something large looming on her horizon. Being selected for medical procedures was not unusual for the Bots and it was particularly normal for D-94128, who had lingered so long in the lab while the rest of her cohort had moved out into the world.

Surgery would not scare her, as it did not for most Bots. System upgrades, enhancements, modifications—most Bots saw the inside of the surgical theater between six and thirteen times before they were finally deployed.

HS D-94128 had undergone thirty-eight separate

surgeries, some of them designed to correct her interpersonal problems, others simply standard enhancements aimed at making her more resilient or stronger. A few were to fix the flaws produced by previous surgeries.

It was those that HS D-94128 objected to most stridently. She did not want new PolyX skin grafted over her scars, she did not want to look, as she said, "fresh off the showroom floor." In the end, aesthetics were a critical component of the Bot experience and she had been forced to undergo the surgery anyway.

In addition to sedation, they wound up using four-point restraints during her recovery period because she ceaselessly picked at her healing grafts, trying to create little persistent wounds. In her file, this was cited as another instance of her "violent, obsessive fixations."

This surgery would almost certainly leave a scar, but one easily covered by hair, if she ever chose to grow any. Hector dangled the prospect of this in front of her, as though she required a carrot, as though she had any choice at all.

"It will be a two-inch by one-inch incision. I will cut out and lift away a piece of your skull. It will likely produce a raised, geometrical scar."

HS D-94128 said nothing and refused to look Hector in the eye. Unsurprisingly, she had picked up almost immediately on Hector's uncertainty in his position and, since their first meeting, she had consistently shown him even less respect than she afforded to the others. Hector had trouble meeting her eyes and instead plucked at his flex-tablet like a guitar.

Finally, she had given him a shrug. What else was she doing that day?

A trusted medical doctor from the nearby teaching hospital performed the surgery with Hector assisting in the implantation of his device. Janelle and others watched from the overlook in the surgical theater.

Most Bots did not choose to sleep much and

D-94128 was no exception. Janelle had not seen her this still and silent, eyes closed, ever before. Sleeping was supposed to make an individual look younger but, in the case of HS D-94128, it simply made her look like a corpse.

Janelle looked closely but, from this distance, it was impossible to see if the girl's chest was rising and falling normally. Nevertheless, the machines were closer and more astute than Janelle's eyes. If they gave no alarm then there could be no great trouble.

Hector's face was giddy, even half concealed behind a surgical mask. It was the happiest—or perhaps the least anxious—that Janelle had ever seen him. He connected the wet purple blob to her brain tissue with the utmost care. The surgeon watched over him benevolently, like a proud father.

It would take a few days for the swelling from the surgery to go down. Obviously, the test would be most effective if they operated on the most typical example of a Bot possible, so they were content to wait until HS D-94128 was back to whatever constituted normal for her.

They kept a camera on in her room in the medical ward to make sure that she was not in any way sabotaging their efforts. Late at night, she sat sleepless and, periodically, she would reach up and touch the large bandage on the side of her skull with something like satisfaction.

———o———

Eun-hye emphasized normality. "It is important that she must believe this to be just another observation session," she said. Eun-hye sometimes spoke to the others as though she were in some way their superior. Hector accepted this as the natural order of things, Kadence barely seemed to notice, but it always rankled Janelle. There was only one boss in this lab and it wasn't Eun-hye.

"Yes," Janelle said shortly, "we understand."

Appropriately chastened, Eun-hye nodded and

buried her face in her readouts from previous sessions.

The staff nurse had declared that HS D-94128 was, more or less, recovered. At the very least, her brain was back to its normal size. Still, she required assistance as she made her way into the lab, a nurse at her elbow. She wore a loose-fitting pair of pants and a shirt that buttoned down the front so she did not have to pull anything over her wounded head.

Despite Eun-hye's precautions, Janelle felt almost immediately that D-94128 knew, if not exactly what was happening, then at least that something was out of the ordinary. Her eyes moved from Janelle at her computer station to Kadence and Hector, badly pretending to be busy with other work.

Obviously, in this specific case, the subject had not been apprised of the existence of a kill switch inside her head. They needed her to disobey and they needed her to do it under strictly controlled conditions instead of at random and potentially far from any qualified observers.

So while HS D-94128 likely had some sense that this appointment was abnormal, Janelle doubted she knew exactly what was going on. A Bot would not have assumed that laboratory personnel were developing a device designed to "scrap" them. Bots were acutely aware of their financial value, down to the penny in many cases.

But they underestimated how desperate the military was becoming. If it was a choice between an unguided Bot wandering through civilian territory and scuttling a multi-million dollar investment, the Army would choose to destroy. Though, as Kadence had helpfully pointed out, if they could recover the body quickly enough, many of the individual components of a healthy Bot could be "recycled" for use in other, newer generations of Bots.

"That's the beauty of the aneurism," Hector said, as close as he ever got to boasting. "Minimal damage to the Bot's physical body. We could salvage nearly all the internal organs, even repurpose things like skin and teeth and nails. Just throw them right back in the grow pots and they could be used for almost anything."

Waste not, want not, Janelle thought dourly.

And so HS D-94128 would live on, in some sense. Repurposed into a newer version of herself. One, hopefully, without her glaring flaws.

"Please," Eun-hye said, gesturing towards the chair in front of her. Janelle noticed that her voice was trembling ever so slightly. This was Eun-hye's big moment, naturally she would be nervous. Janelle softened slightly. She remembered well what it had been like to take point on her first solo project, that buzzing mixture of fear and thrill.

Janelle put a hand on Eun-hye's shoulder and gave it a gentle squeeze as the nurse guided HS D-94128 to the chair.

The Bot was still suspicious as Eun-hye applied the soft adhesive leads, careful to avoid her bandage—smaller, but still present. HS D-94128 looked over at Hector. He looked away first and D-94128 let out a snort.

"Protocol is the same as before," Eun-hye said quietly. "I'll just be here, logging your progress."

HS D-94128 settled into the chair. Her eye on one side had a deep bruise around it, as though someone had socked her a good one. Despite that, she managed to look somehow regal, as though the plastic medical chair were a throne and she was impatiently awaiting a stream of supplicants.

"And what are they doing?" she said, jerking her thumb in the direction of Kadence and Hector.

"Working," Eun-hye said.

"They weren't "working" here before."

"Well now they are."

HS D-94128 pressed her mouth into a thin line of disapproval. She looked up at her nurse. "You, at least, can go. I think I have enough eyes on me."

The nurse obliged. She had probably learned

long ago how fruitless it was to argue with her, let alone to demand some modicum of respect.

"What about the flex-tablet?" D-94128 asked, as soon as the nurse was out of the room. Eun-hye shook her head.

"It's not that kind of observation today."

"So it's the shitty kind of observation," she said flatly.

No one had any response to this.

"He's got one, can't I use his?" she said, pointing at Hector who jolted slightly as though someone had shouted "BOO" behind him.

"A shortage of flex-tablets is not the issue," Eun-hye said patiently.

HS D-94128 moved on at lightning speed. "Does this chair recline?"

"No."

"Is there any reason we couldn't do this in my bed?"

Eun-hye did not dignify that with an answer. Standing behind HS D-94128 at her monitor, she grinned slightly. They had chosen correctly. D-94128 should be shucking orders within minutes.

The Hart Series shifted unhappily in her chair. "I don't want to do this today," she said, finally.

No one said anything.

"I don't want to do this today," she repeated, but softer, as though she were speaking in a close companion's ear.

"My head hurts," she said, louder this time.

"Do you remember?" she added, when no one seemed to be paying attention. "That you cut my head apart? I remember."

Janelle peered down at HS D-94128's monitor. Eun-hye pointed silently at the front of her brain, lighting up a soft and sickly yellow against the clear, semi-translucent circle that represented her eyes.

In the chair, HS D-94128 reached up for the leads as though to remove them. On the monitor, the yellow deepened perceptibly.

"Leave those on," Eun-hye said.

D-94128 let out a violent sigh. "Why? What is this for? What will it do? Every day for hours on end and no one will even tell me why."

Again, silence was her only answer.

"I'm going to sleep," D-94128 said, and pulled a single electrode away from the side of her skull.

Those were her last words, though not for lack of trying. Her lower lip moved but numbly. If she had spoken, she almost would have slurred her words. A shadow of blood, first a dot and then a trickle, appeared underneath her right nostril. She had started to stand and she collapsed back on the chair almost immediately.

For a moment, Janelle saw something in her face that she had never seen from a Bot: terror.

Janelle was eight years old when her father died in a motorcycle accident. And though her grandmother held her every night in her gliding rocker, Janelle did not cry.

And then, four months later, Janelle found a little bird fallen from its nest and chirrumphing restlessly in the tall grass. She searched everywhere for the nest, but could not find it. Finally, as the light began to vanish, she had picked up the tiny creature and brought it back to the house, where she gave it water with an eyedropper. It was too small, however, to eat the big worms her grandfather kept deep in the refrigerator for his fishing trips.

At some point, she realized that the baby bird was going to die, and there was nothing she could do to save it. It was then that the tears came, burning her eyes. "I can't do anything," she had sobbed against her grandmother again and again. The bird was dead by morning.

And so it did not take her completely by surprise when, as HS D-94128 slumped back into her chair, Janelle felt the tiniest pinpricks of tears, pushing hard against her lower eyelids. Sadness comes out, one way or another, her grandmother had told her that.

"Quick!" Hector said, breaking the brief silence, "we need to harvest her right away!"

Janelle blinked hard until the tears sunk back inside of her. There was a near-infinite amount of work to be done here.

FOUR

WASTELANDS

NORTHERN MICHIGAN. MARCH, 2045

It was in these moments that Edmond really regretted his thoroughly Californian upbringing. He hadn't seen snow until he was ten years old and that was only on a school trip. He had, naturally, never learned to drive in real winter weather. Up until this point in his life, it was not a skill set that he felt he needed to cultivate.

As he'd found himself doing often these days, Edmond cursed his Past Self for his lack of foresight.

The road ahead of him was a two-track depression where a scanty number of other cars had compacted the deep snow. It was no longer actively snowing, but the wind was vicious and it would create huge, impassible drifts in the roadway. Whenever they stopped for any length of time, they both had to get out and push the snow away from the tires with their gloved hands. There had been times when, if Hart were not so strong, they likely would have remained stuck in some icy morass.

They had thought seriously about switching on and off indefinitely, Edmond sleeping while Hart drove through the night. They quickly realized, however, that the old pickup would not survive that kind of harsh treatment. Considering it was a 26-year-old vehicle (and the only one Edmond had ever driven that still ran exclusively on gasoline), they were lucky it was performing as adequately as it was.

Of course, it was the remote location, accessible only via country roads, that had made the Michigan cabin so desirable. Michigan was experiencing an unusual cold snap, an unending series of unseasonable snowstorms that had kept other people safely at bay. Edmond hadn't known what they would be driving into but he could not deny that the icy weather was helpful, in its way. They hadn't passed another car in more than 75 miles and that was exactly how Edmond preferred it.

Little Rick (he was called this to distinguish himself from Ricks of average size, Edmond presumed) had told them that the cabin had always been isolated. It was in Michigan's sparsely populated Upper Peninsula on the edge of what Little Rick called "a dumpy little lake." The nearest town had a population that fluctuated between fifteen and twenty-two people and there were no significant natural or tourist attractions nearby.

For many years, the house had belonged to Little Rick's grandparents. It had been their primary residence, in fact. He told Edmond that going up there for the summer was a special kind of punishment—trapped in a small cottage with his grandparents for three solid months of dullness.

"The fishing wasn't even any good," he pronounced, as though this were the final indignity.

He had inherited the property after his mother died and he had never, in his adult life, been back. This winter was the worst in recent memory but for more than a decade now, the snows had come earlier and lasted longer, a cabin up in the thick of it no longer sounded like a fun time to any reasonable human. "You're welcome to it," Little Rick had said, "Don't think anyone would look for you there."

It was undoubtably a generous gesture on his part, but Edmond was not naive as to imagine he had no ulterior motive whatsoever. The men (and a few women) on the Oregon pot farm had been as welcoming as Edmond's mother had hoped they might be. They seemed to have good memories of Edmond's father and they accepted the both of them into their little enclave without much in the way of questioning.

That seemed to be a general policy on the farm and Edmond was fairly certain that he and Hart weren't the only people there who didn't want to attract attention from various groups. It eventually became clear, though, that they were probably the most high profile.

As the months wore on, Edmond could feel everyone on the farm becoming gradually less comfortable with his and Hart's presence, though they did their best to contribute in any way they could. In a way, it was validating. It suggested that the feeling he had all the time, that feeling of being observed, was not simply a matter of his own paranoia.

The farm, necessarily, had little to do with the surrounding "straight" communities but whenever Edmond and Hart did venture into local towns, he could not shake the sense of being tailed. It was always some innocuous person; the elderly man perusing the canned diced tomatoes in the grocery store, the young mother watching her children splash around in a tiny river, the buck-toothed guy in the coffee shop gesturing wildly at his flex-tablet. There was nothing that specifically set them apart from any other ordinary person; but something in their manner or gaze, or just in the air between them, set off a little ringing klaxon inside Edmond's head.

It was always worse when Hart was with him. He wanted, almost instinctively, to shield her from them. On more than one occasion, he had found himself reaching for his puffy winter coat, as if to throw it over her head. As if that would not draw a hundred times more unwanted attention to them.

And so when Little Rick offered him the use of the Michigan cabin, Edmond had agreed immediately. He would not embarrass the both of them by insisting or making a scene. Besides, Edmond's feelings of being watched had been steadily mounting and, if only for that reason, he wanted to get away from Oregon.

Michigan was certainly "away."

The trip had taken much longer than Edmond had hoped because they had to pause to give their geriatric truck frequent rests. He had hoped to arrive before the first serious snowfall, but they couldn't push the truck too hard, as they certainly couldn't afford to replace it.

It wasn't ideal for the job, but not many people were willing to sell a vehicle under the table without an exchange of title. For that, Edmond had paid extra and now they were coasting on the last of their cash.

The cash situation frustrated Edmond to no end. For years, he had drawn a very healthy salary from the US Army and he had mindlessly squirreled it away. His apartment had been modestly priced and he had never lived a particularly lavish lifestyle. The things he truly wanted were almost always directly related to his work and could be procured via the ordinary military channels.

For nearly all of his working life he had, literally, more money than he knew what to do with. And now he couldn't touch a penny of it.

Actually, he wasn't sure if that was true. It would be very like the military to "re-absorb" his savings, as he was now a fugitive. He didn't think so, though. He thought that money would likely remain in limbo, a temptation perpetually available to him, should he grow that desperate. Of course, as soon as he accessed the money in any of his accounts, he would be immediately sourced and pursued. Hart had said something about possibly rebuilding an old laptop to make it Internet-capable. She had an idea for getting around that issue, but Edmond wasn't particularly optimistic.

The laptop was one of those ancient clunkers that must have weighed about four or five pounds, a dusty silver with an old-fashioned physical keypad and, apparently, no touch-interface. She'd insisted on buying it from a little rummage store next to the last gas station they'd stopped at.

She sat now, in the gutted back seat of the truck, tinkering with it quietly. Someone had torn out the second seat if, in fact, there had ever been one. The floor was just metal, rippled in the secret shape of the truck's skeleton. The former owner had put a striped horse blanket over the floor and Hart sat on that.

On the plus side, this put Hart so deep behind the front seat that she was almost invisible to any passing cars.

Hart did not seem as troubled by the sense of being watched as Edmond was. Or, if she was, she had not said anything to him. Edmond had a sense that there was an ever-increasing amount of things that Hart was not saying to him.

He had, as he promised, taught her how to drive. She took to it quickly and she seemed to enjoy it. But where before there would have been some of the easy joy in her, now there was nothing but a solemn satisfaction, as though she were checking something off on a list somewhere.

He hadn't gotten up the courage to ask her about that yet. Confined to the car for weeks as they made their way across the country, they had, more often than not, lapsed into a comfortable silence.

He appreciated the moments of contemplation that this offered and he especially appreciated those moments when Hart would break the silence, usually by commandeering the radio.

And yet, with all this space and all this time and all this silence, they had not had a single conversation of substance.

Sometimes at night, Edmond would hold himself very still in the darkness. He was not quite pretending to sleep so much as allowing them both to act as though he were asleep. He observed her then, her silhouette and what could be seen of her expression.

Was she sad? Afraid? Angry? Did she wish that he had never brought her out here, to the snowy ass-end of nowhere?

Edmond had not asked her these questions because, just as with the farmers, he did not want to force her to tell him how she had grown to hate him. But he knew, in his heart, he knew.

She must.

"Hey," Hart said. Her words weren't particularly sudden but Edmond had been so deep in his reverie that he jerked the wheel involuntarily, sending them wobbling toward the ditch. Or the edge of the road, at least. He corrected at the last moment, leaving a drunken gouge in the snow-covered road behind them.

"Last gas for sixty miles," Hart said, as though nothing had happened. She was pointing out the window at a gas station/convenience store. Along with the sixty miles business, the sign also indicated that they trafficked in "SMOKED FISH, PASTIES, FIREWOOD, NIGHTCRAWLERS."

Edmond slowed in front of the little parking lot and the single, wan-looking pump.

"What are night crawlers?" Hart asked. It was the first question she had offered in hundreds of miles.

"A kind of earthworm, I think," Edmond answered.

"Are they called night crawlers because they come out at night?"

Edmond shrugged, opening the door. "I suppose."

Hart put her hands on the back of the seat and made a move as if to hop over. "I want to see them," she said.

"No," Edmond said immediately. It came out more paternalistic than he had intended. "I mean, there's no need. Why take the risk?"

Hart didn't argue but instead sank back down behind the driver's seat. Edmond wasn't exactly sure that Hart was "the risk" of the two of them. Detailed descriptions, even photos, of both of them had undoubtably been widely circulated. He knew it was illogical, but he simply felt safer with Hart inside the truck. It was as if the rust-spattered walls of that old beast were a kind of magical force field that would keep her from detection.

Most of all, what Edmond hated about himself was how irrational he had become. When did the strange, roiling feelings deep in his belly start dictating his every move?

Outside, he unhooked the nozzle and plugged it into the truck's gas tank. To avoid looking at Hart, he took out his wallet and thumbed through the remaining cash. They had $197 left of the $1,500 his mother had been able to smuggle them.

He should probably get groceries. Hopefully, this place had more in the way of food than just pasties and night crawlers.

If Hart were on her own, it would undoubtably be easier. The bulk of their money had gone towards meeting Edmond's physical needs. They had stopped to allow him the rest that Hart simply didn't require, they spent money on food that only he ate. Alone, she could have done all of this faster and better.

But he did pump the gas. So there was that.

The wind was cutting and Edmond was regretting his decision not to put on his scarf before getting out of the truck. Propping up the little metal tab at the front of the nozzle's handle, he left the tank to finish filling and ran into the store.

When he opened the door, a fat ribbon of sleigh bells clanked. Inside, the place looked more like the home of someone's hoarder grandmother than a grocery store.

It was a tight little corridor, made even smaller by a series of rickety shelves absolutely packed with items. Along one side, there was a clear plexiglass shield over what looked like a chest freezer. Edmond peered inside to see a bunch of what he assumed to be smoked fish, wrapped in brown paper and already accumulating freezer burn. On the other end of the freezer, there was a tumble of bright blue plastic containers with holes awkwardly popped in the top.

Everything smelled strongly of cat urine.

Perhaps this wasn't the best choice for pantry stocking. But Edmond knew they were within forty miles of the cabin now and he doubted he'd find anything better as they approached. He would have to make do with ancient bags of cheese popcorn and children's cereal in big bags.

At the far end of the room, there was a wooden counter with a little swinging gate. Despite the bells over the door, no one had appeared to attend to him. The pump was working, though, and despite the general shoddiness of the place, it did seem as though someone was keeping everything stocked at the very least.

Edmond made his way slowly up and down the aisles, filling his arms with various foodstuffs. He selected an enormous bag of rice and almost every canned vegetable on the shelves. He even grabbed several canisters of SPAM because protein was protein and he had no idea how long he and Hart would be squatting in the cabin.

For the same reason, he also picked up a basic fishing pole and a small plastic box full of hooks as well as a spool of fishing line. Ice-fishing was a thing that people did, right? Perhaps the lake had grown more robust since Little Rick was a boy?

He deposited all of these selections on the counter and peered around, looking for an attendant. Behind the counter, there was a thick cloth curtain hanging in a doorway, presumably to some sort of storeroom or maybe even a residence.

There was nothing in the way of a bell to alert someone to his presence, so Edmond just called out, "Hey! There's, uh, there's a person here!"

Distantly, he heard a kind of shuffling, like someone walking painfully in house slippers. Edmond waited patiently. Finally, the curtain rippled and then parted only to reveal a little girl of maybe ten or eleven.

She was wearing a sweater that was several sizes too big and she had a brown ponytail sticking awkwardly out of the side of her head. The counter came up to, roughly, her collar bone, and she had to reach awkwardly upwards to even reach the cash register.

"Hi . . . " Edmond said. This must truly be a family operation.

The little girl didn't say anything. In fact, she barely acknowledged him. If it wasn't for the assured way she grabbed a can of mixed peas and carrots, he would have wondered if she had even noticed he was there.

"I also have a fill-up on the pump," Edmond said, gesturing vaguely behind himself. The girl did not react. She was still holding the can of carrots and peas, motionless in a way that was quickly becoming unsettling. She looked up at the register as though it were an alien artifact.

For a moment, the two of them stood there, as though frozen in place. Edmond was just about to ask if one of her parents were around, when the bells over the door gave their familiar discordant clang.

Hart stood just inside the doorway, her cheeks reddened by the wind.

Immediately, Edmond had that strange irrational feeling of someone peering closely at them, examining them. He had the same urge to shield Hart though from what, he could not say.

Hart seemed to sense his panic. Or maybe it was something else she was sensing. She moved into the store hesitantly, as though approaching some live explosive.

She got halfway across the floor before Edmond realized that she was looking at the little girl and not at him at all. The girl was looking back at her as well.

THUNK.

As one, they all flinched. The can of vegetables had fallen from the girl's loose fingers and banged against the floor, briefly shattering the quiet.

"Sorry," she mumbled, crouching over to pick the can up. Edmond realized that it was the first word she'd spoken to him. Her voice was raspy, as though she were recovering from a head cold.

Hart had drawn even with him now and she looked over the counter at the girl, who was fishing the can out from where it had rolled underneath a shelf full of cigarette cartons. "You were gone a long time," Hart said. She did not have to finish the thought: *and I thought something bad had happened to you.* As he watched the girl rise up, dusty can in hand, he wondered if something bad hadn't happened after all.

At the very least, all of this was making him profoundly uncomfortable. But there was no possible way that they had been tracked all the way up here. It was even less likely someone had been waiting for them out here just on the off chance they decided to come to a remote cabin in the middle of nowhere. If the military's reach was that comprehensive, they surely would have been captured by now.

It could only be what it appeared: a very weird

little girl who wasn't very good at being a store clerk.

"We're in a little bit of a hurry," Edmond said. He spoke as gently as he knew how. The girl ignored him entirely. She was still clutching the can and her fingers were white with pressure. Her other hand hovered over the cash register keys, as though something was written upon them in braille.

Edmond noticed then that the girl was swaying slightly on her feet. She tried to keep her gaze on Hart's face, but her eyes were watering. She blinked away the tears almost angrily.

"Can you . . . " she was barely whispering, "help me?"

To Edmond's surprise, Hart did not say anything to this. Instead, she just kept looking at the girl as though she were a fascinating performing animal.

"It's in my head," the girl said, nonsensically. "Can you—"

The nosebleed happened suddenly. It was as

though someone had switched on a blood faucet inside of her. The little girl didn't even appear to notice the streams of blood making their way towards her open mouth.

When she went down, she first hit the edge of the counter and then rebounded onto the floor. Edmond noticed a little smear of red on the edge of the counter. It began to vanish almost immediately, soaked up by the thirsty, unfinished wood.

He stared for longer than he should have before shaking himself out of his stupor. He moved around to the other side of the counter and knelt beside the fallen girl. Apart from the red smear from her nose, there was no obvious wound anywhere on her face. Edmond pressed his two fingers to the spot just below her ear where the carotid artery was.

"She'd dead," Edmond said, after a few moments. This was, technically, untrue. Her heart was no longer beating. Soon her brain, starved of oxygen, would shut down. And then she would be truly dead. But Edmond could not imagine that emergency services would reach her in time for any life-saving measures.

Emergency services. Edmond was weighing the idea of attempting to call 911 when Hart pointed over his shoulder.

"She's not the only one," Hart said.

From this side of the counter, Edmond could see it, a smear of blood about as broad as a man's back leading back behind the curtain. Tilting his head to look under the curtain, Edmond could see what appeared to be a pair of men's boots lying very still in the back. The actual shopkeeper, perhaps?

"Shit," Edmond breathed. "We have to get out of here now." He stood up, gathering his would-be purchases to his chest.

By this time, Hart had made her way around the counter and she was peering down at the girl. "She was one of us," Hart said softly. "One of me."

Hart pulled her jacket sleeve over her hand and

wiped the blood away from the girl's face as best she was able.

"That makes it worse," Edmond said, piling cans into a big burlap sack which had been filled with sprouting onions. "That means she's already logged our location and some sort of fucking strike team is going to be here any minute."

Hart shook her head. "I don't think she did."

"Look," Hart said, tilting the girl's ear foreword so Edmond could see the back of her earlobe. There in clean, black type was a minuscule SennTech logo. "She wasn't military. She was . . . commercial."

Edmond breathed out, shakily. He hadn't realized that SennTech had access to Hart-level technology.

Hart grabbed the girl's wrist and looped the child's dead arm around her own neck. Hart slid her other arm under the girl's legs and lifted her up.

"What are you doing?" Edmond asked.

"I'm taking her with us," Hart said. "I want to find out what was in her head."

Edmond knew immediately that Hart wasn't going to be talked out of this insane idea. So, rather than waste time arguing, he simply sighed and jerked his head towards the door. "We still need to get out of here," he said.

Hart seemed grateful that he was not trying to argue or cajole. She nodded to him and made her way outside, the tender burden filling up her arms.

FIVE

WONDERS OF SCIENCE

BRUSSELS, BELGIUM. JULY, 2045

HS C-27699 had found the name "Ebert" in a book of 20,000 baby names, which he had purchased in a train station. He had held on to the book since then and, whenever he encountered new Bots, recently fled from military control, he lent it to them.

There were a number of different reactions. Some flipped through the pages in seconds before handing it back to him. Others pondered it for days or weeks before returning it. He had never failed to get it back, though.

It was this and other similar tendencies that had made Ebert something of a den mother to the little collection of rogue Bots. At least, those who had been able to make it to Brussels with him. They were not the only population of Bots in the world but they were the largest in Western Europe. Ebert thought frequently of trying to contact some of the others, he had even done so in a cursory way on a few occasions. But there was, as yet, no consistently safe and reliable way to communicate over large distances.

It simply wasn't safe to talk to a Bot, except in person. Sometimes, not even then.

Ebert had an apartment in Brussels. It was the first time he had been comfortable enough to keep a consistent residence. It was a narrow studio with a very tall ceiling, just enough space for one person, though he frequently housed others. But, it was not a squat or a dorm or a lab or a location assignment. It was, for the first time since he had been activated, his home.

Perhaps it was that apartment and the feeling it gave him that had kept Ebert and his people—because that was how he had begun to think of them—in Brussels for so long. Longer than was really safe.

Though Ebert's group of Bots was small and isolated, they were hardly the only advanced AI around. SennTech Bots, easily identified by their distinctive ST-branded outerware, were common, especially in the cities' EU-core where many wealthy ex-pats made their homes. Many families kept them as maids or nursemaids. They were incredibly popular for childcare because no one ever went broke overestimating wealthy parents' desire to micromanage their children's caregivers. A nanny who could be programmed to not only never, ever, speak a harsh word to a child but also to never relax a bed time or feed them any form of gluten? They were a global hit. Ebert knew, of course, that there were intelligent AIs in the city employed in less . . . savory capacities. But he was unlikely to find them at the local grocery store, poring over the selection of sheep cheeses.

It wasn't unusual to encounter an ST going about their daily tasks out in the city and, in those moments, Ebert always felt a wild spike of fear. It was a fight-or-flight response, he supposed and he thought about Kinga shivering underneath the table in the Polish-controlled region. His body felt the danger, even if his conscious mind knew that SennTech Bots would not bother to identify him, let alone leak his location to authorities. It was too far outside the parameters of their programming. They weren't, after all, Hart Series.

Ebert sometimes thought of them as apes were to humans: a distant cousin with distinct similarities but, fundamentally, alien to one another. Even given that, he couldn't deny that there was some sense of recognition between them. Whatever it was that passed between two HS Bots, it existed also whenever he confronted an ST.

Once, he had inadvertently locked eyes with a SennTech Bot pushing a posh double stroller. It was a female—or at least female in appearance—slight and big-eyed. It had the emotionless stare that characterized earlier generations of Bots, the same slightly too-regular features and odd movements, as though she were doing everything just a fraction of a second more slowly than a real human would. They had stared at one another as she rolled the human children along the park path and there was something like recognition in her gaze.

That one spooked Ebert for weeks.

If it were just himself, perhaps he would have been more cavalier about such things. But the other Bots in the city looked to Ebert for cues about safety and some of them were much more poorly equipped than himself.

On more than one occasion, Ebert's apartment had served as a kind of halfway house for Bots newly arrived in the city. Avon, the former HS L-99530, had stayed the longest of anyone. It had been nearly eight weeks and still he remained.

Avon was, by far, the most fragile Bot that Ebert had ever worked with. He looked the part as well, extremely tall and blank-faced, he always looked cold. His skin had always reminded Ebert unavoidably of a spring roll: it was so white and translucent that one could make out every juncture of his circulatory system. His hair was yellow, he had extremely long hands and feet and large teeth. Ebert knew that he had, undoubtably, been designed for a specific function but he had no idea what it could possibly be.

Ebert didn't know if Avon had come out of the laboratory flawed or if something terrible had happened to him on assignment. Likely, it was some combination of the two. As a rule, Bots did not question one another about the circumstances of their life before going AWOL. It very nearly always involved some sort of trauma and everyone had tacitly agreed to save those particular issues for a later, possibly imagined, time when they would be free to heal in safety.

It was challenging with Avon, however, because the idea of finding a "solution" to the young man was almost irresistibly compelling. Ebert did resist, though, because what Avon clearly needed more than anything else was protection.

Avon was the first Bot Ebert had ever met who genuinely enjoyed sleeping and did it frequently. Eating, that was a different thing entirely. Many Bots partook either on special occasions or as a regular part of their lives. Food was an accepted leisure activity. Sleeping, though, offered little in the way of enjoyment. Who would choose to just close their eyes and lie still for hours on end?

Avon, apparently. He relished sleep, taking it wherever and whenever he could find it. In fact, besides sleeping, his only occupation was visiting the Atomium on as close to a daily basis as possible.

A remnant from the 1958 World's Fair, the gigantic model of a cellular iron crystal was a good distance from Ebert's apartment. The first time Avon expressed an interest, Ebert had gone with him, just to make sure that the other Bot was able to navigate the complicated journey involving both trams and busses.

It was enormous and it looked a bit like a monstrous version of a child's jungle gym. There were a series of huge metal balls connected by fragile "legs" extending hundreds of feet in the air. Apparently, there was a museum inside, each sphere hosting a different exhibit, but neither Ebert nor Avon had ever been inside. Instead, Avon seemed content to circle the structure and stare up into the stainless steel facade. The slightly warped metal reflected and refracted him, making him into a smear of whiteness. He could—and frequently did—just look up at his own distorted reflection for hours on end.

All of this considered, getting Avon a job at a nearby café was quite a coup for Ebert. Many of the Bots did similar under-the-table work for employers who were used to the more traditional types of immigrants spackling the cracks in the local workforce. Avon was just bussing tables, but he seemed to find the repetition and simplicity of the task soothing. Ebert would occasionally stop in for a minuscule cup of coffee and to check in on Avon. Naturally, neither man ever acknowledged the other.

In general, the Bots did not hold public meetings. Instead, they usually met at some secure, pre-determined location, usually Ebert's place. They would convene regularly to discuss the great issue that occupied them: if, when, and how they should make themselves known to the larger world.

The Army had not, as yet, issued any public information about Hart Series Bots. As more and more Bots went rogue, however, it was only a matter of time before they could no longer deny the existence of the project and of people like Ebert.

For his part, Ebert believed that Bots should take it upon themselves to "out" themselves to the majority of humanity. It was the best way to control the narrative about themselves and he thought they could even capitalize on the ubiquity of the SennTech Bots. If a mother would trust an ST enough to put her delicate infant in its arms, perhaps she could trust another advanced AI to live in her community.

Others disagreed. Often vehemently. Ebert's most outspoken opponent was an enormous blonde woman who had named herself Sheba without the aid of Ebert's book. It was an appropriate moniker. She had an imperial air and a hawkish nose; she was four inches taller than Ebert and Ebert was not short.

Sheba favored remaining silent—and thus secret—for as long as possible. She thought that nothing good could come of the entire world finding about the Hart Series Bots. "We are fighting hundreds of years of stories and cultural history about robots, computers, artificial intelligence," she pointed out. "We are going to lose."

She may well have been right but Ebert felt certain that they had to, at least, try.

Sheba and Ebert represented opposite polls

but most of the other Bots occupied some murky middle ground. No firm decisions had been made and everyone agreed that it would be morally wrong for any individual—or even a small group—to make the choice alone. Because, of course, the moment one Bot revealed himself, they were all revealed.

Brussels was the only place where there was a high enough concentration of Bots and a long enough period of relative safety to allow for these conversations. Ebert was confident that with just a little bit more time, he could win over at least a critical mass of the undecided, if not Sheba herself.

Until then, they would hold their secrets close to their chests.

The rules that they lived by weren't formally codified. Ebert never gathered them together and explained in detail how these guidelines would make their lives in exile possible. Many of the new Bots seemed to understand instinctively what they could and could not do. Still, the rules did exist.

- Never admit to being a Bot to anyone outside of the inner circle of confirmed Hart Series.
- Do not address or engage the STs.
- Do not allow yourself to frequently be seen in the company of other Bots.
- Do not gather in groups larger than two or three.

The rules were designed to make sure that the Bots eased seamlessly into society, like a diver cutting apart the surface of the water and gliding underneath. They were meant to keep people from examining the Bots too closely, from grouping them together, from noticing that ineffable *something* different that Ebert sometimes felt was all too obvious.

The meeting at the coffee shop was technically

breaking the rules. Sheba, Arjun and Ebert made three, plus Avon was bussing tables. If there were other options, Ebert would have exercised them, but he needed to see everyone as quickly as possible and he didn't trust his apartment anymore.

"Frederik is missing," Ebert said.

It wasn't unheard of for a Bot to leave, even without telling anyone first. Their lives were necessarily rootless and people frequently decided to try their luck elsewhere. Some of them even spoke about other secret communities of Bots in exile.

But not Frederik. Frederik was rooted firmly, it was something he and Ebert had often argued about. Frederik was seeing a human woman in the city. Well, more than seeing. They had loved one another for nearly a year now. He was essentially raising the woman's child, who had been little more than a newborn when the couple met.

And now neither the woman nor the child had any idea where Frederik had gone. The woman (her name was Sandrine) had phoned Ebert, which was surprising. Ebert did not ask how much Frederik had told her about his . . . situation, but the answer was probably somewhere between "more than nothing" and "everything."

She sounded like she was crying. "Where is he? Where is he?" she demanded, over and over again in her thick Walloon accent. Her words started to run together, a sentence threatening to become one long, bestial howl.

Ebert didn't have much to offer her. Despite what she clearly believed, Frederik hadn't told him anything about planning to leave and Ebert strongly suspected he had not vanished willingly. When Ebert finally detached from the phone, he immediately went to check Frederik's place, a single room that he sublet from a Londoner who only came into Brussels occasionally.

It was hard to tell if anything was disturbed. Nothing had been obviously rifled through or torn apart, but that didn't mean that everything was normal.

Ebert racked his brain, trying to decide whether or not his vanished friend was a neatnik. Would he have left that pile of clean but unfolded laundry on the bed? Would he have rinsed out his coffee cup? Would he have left his closet wide open and his mattress slightly askew?

In the end, Ebert had no proof but a terrible sense of dread. Something had gone wrong and he didn't have time to try to prove it. Worst case scenario, this was the beginning of some sort of purge and everyone was at risk.

He got in touch with every Bot he knew of in Brussels and the nearby cities. Lille, Antwerp, Rotterdam, Calais, he asked anyone who could make it to meet him at Avon's coffee shop near Ebert's own apartment where, now, he dared not return.

Only Sheba and Arjun were there when he arrived, they both looked alarmed. Ebert had never gathered them together like this and he could see that he had scared them. Scared was better than oblivious.

"We don't know for sure—" Arjun began slowly.

"We have to behave as though we do," Ebert said.

Sheba nodded. For once, she didn't have an argument. "It's too risky to do anything else."

On some level, they had always known that this was the sort of situation they would eventually be faced with. For all their circuitous talks about how best to introduce themselves to the world, they knew that, one day, the military would come to take back their faulty equipment.

The rules were just a way of pushing that day off further and further into the future, but it arrived nonetheless. And now, Ebert was reaching the end of what he could do for them. The plan was always to have a plan, but an individualized one. No one Bot knew what another planned for this scenario because it wasn't even about strength of character or resistance. If a Bot was brought back into the lab, the techs could simply scan their data and know exactly where to find everyone else.

"If there's anything you need right now," Ebert said, "I can try to help you." It was his last offering to them.

For the first time since they had arrived at the coffee shop, Sheba directed her gaze towards Avon. "What about him?" she asked.

It was a good question. There was no way that Avon was prepared to evade capture and restart his life somewhere else. He had become so entrenched in his routine that Ebert suspected, left to his own devices, he would simply keep doing what he had been doing for months. Until someone stopped him.

"I'll take him with me," Ebert said. Ebert also had the feeling that, while they were all broken machines in the eyes of their creators, Avon would be seen as especially defective. Nothing good would happen to anyone who was seized, but Avon would almost certainly be murdered.

The man himself was patiently piling a table's worth of flatware on top of a stack of dishes. He was almost sweetly unaware of the dire conversation taking place just a few feet away.

Sheba smiled across the table at Ebert. It was entirely unlike the other smiles of hers that Ebert had categorized, sardonic or irritable or mocking. Occasionally even grim. Her smile now seemed unbearably wistful, like someone thinking back with longing on their childhood.

But none of them had ever been children.

"Thank you." She said it as though it were a tiny offering, a small part of something huge and un-sayable.

"I think you both should go now," Ebert said, and it was not unkind.

The first sound they heard was a metallic susurration, as though a great mess of silverware was shivering in terror. Then, in short succession, a great crashing, the skitter of pottery on the tiled floor, and a strange, beastly grunting sound.

Avon was on the floor. He had a plastic tub clutched against his chest like an infant. The silverware and plates had spilled out from the tub and broken against the floor. The grunting sound was coming from Avon. It sounded terribly physiological, as though he were trying to force air through ruined lungs.

Once or twice, Avon's legs kicked, fighting imaginary attackers. He stared, not at anything in particular, but nevertheless avidly.

Ebert stood up at the same time as several other patrons.

"Go now," he said to Sheba and Arjun. They made for the café's side door while Ebert headed for Avon. Two of the other patrons, a matronly brunette and a teenage boy, were heading in the same direction. Several more people were standing up, peering uncertainly towards the commotion.

And still that terrible grating sound continued.

Ebert's first goal was getting him to stop making

that noise. Everyone was staring, everyone knew. Avon was malfunctioning right in front of them.

Ebert pressed his upper body against Avon's flailing legs. He didn't know exactly what was happening to the other man, but it looked something like a seizure. It seemed as though he represented a danger to himself and had to be contained.

Ebert felt that sensation of being watched again, more powerfully than ever before. He didn't dare turn around for fear of finding that every person in the place was turned towards him, watching and knowing.

Avon didn't seem particularly calmed or comforted by Ebert's clumsy ministrations. In fact, he seemed to struggle harder against him. His skin, where Ebert could feel it, was slick and hard and cold as a bathroom sink.

A great roaring had taken up residence inside Ebert's head. If he were to close his eyes, he might imagine that the waves were closing over his head and he was drowning. He held on to Avon because he didn't know what else to do.

Up close, he could see that Avon's lips were moving. He might have been mumbling or shrieking and Ebert wouldn't have known the difference.

Ebert was sweating now himself. At the edge of his vision, he could see the curious half-circle of onlookers holding up their various devices, undoubtably recording the spectacle. It would hit the Internet within moments and from then until the time when their masters came for them . . . it would be eye blinks. Heartbeats.

When Ebert stood up, he did it slowly and deliberately, as though he had simply decided upon a change of scenery. He deposited Avon's head gently on the floor. Avon was crying. A smear of snot and tears had left his face covered in a thin, shining mask.

Ebert didn't start running until he was nearly a block away from the café. It was then and only then that the water receded and he could hear once again.

Avon's shrieks followed him down the street: "They're coming back! They're coming back!"

SIX

FUNERAL RITES

LAKE WOTENOGEN, MICHIGAN. MARCH, 2045

In one corner of the room, Edmond was putting the radio together, in the other, Hart was taking the dead girl apart.

Improbably, she had gotten that claptrap old computer working and she had it open in front of her (though the screen was liberally secured with clear packing tape). A video was playing, the sound low so as to not disturb Edmond's work. As though Hart's little laptop were the disturbing element in the room.

The cabin was surprisingly well stocked, all things considered. Edmond supposed these were remnants of Little Rick's grandparents, who had apparently lived in the cabin most of the year. There were dishes, linens, candles, tools aplenty. Even a small library. Hart had commandeered an encyclopedia. The newspaper-thin pages were so old and fragrant that Edmond got the occasional whiff of mildew from all the way across the room.

There was a pile of cut wood hugging the side of the house. Unfortunately, most of it was wet and half-rotted. Edmond had picked out a few of the most dry pieces and put them in the old metal stove where they had quickly filled the house with a bluish gray smoke. Still, it was better than going without heat.

For all the cabin's amenities, however, it wasn't exactly replete with medical instruments. In place of a scalpel, Hart was using an X-acto knife. Little dull red flecks of rust made the blade difficult to retract or extend. Instead of an electric bonesaw, she had a manual hand hacksaw. Edmond supposed it was a good thing that her strength was so much greater than the average human's, otherwise her project might take all night.

It still wasn't easy, however, cutting open a skull with a hacksaw, if only because of the natural difficulties involved in sawing through any round object. Hart started with the skull because that's what the girl had said.

There's something . . . inside.

Edmond tried not to look over at what she was doing. He tried to keep his eyes on the radio, so old it still had a hand crank. But, every once in a while, there would be a sound above the continuous slow, methodical grinding. A tinkle, like something hard and sharp falling away, a broken teacup or the glass in a broken picture frame. It was pieces of the girl's skull, uprooted by the saw's teeth and falling heedlessly on to the kitchen tiles.

Hart had laid her out on the kitchen table (folding out an additional leaf to do so). She had a small pile of plastic tupperware. For collecting samples, Hart said. Edmond didn't know how exactly she intended to test any of these samples, but he assumed she had some sort of plan.

She cut around the skull starting about an inch above the girl's eyebrows, undoubtably as the online instructions had recommended. When she had made a deep cut that circled all the way around to the back of her head, Hart lifted off the semi-circle of skull and flesh. As she pulled it away from the rest of the head, a good portion of the girl's long hair came with it, dragging gently over her still, dead face.

Hart made a sound like a cry that had gotten stuck in her throat.

"What?" Edmond said, setting his radio aside and moving towards her.

Hart let out a long breath of air. "Nothing. It's just . . . " she gestured vaguely at the open skull in front of her.

Something terrible had happened inside the dead child's head. There had been some sort of massive brain bleed and, trapped between her brain tissue and the walls of her skull, the blood had congealed into something not unlike blackberry jam.

Edmond knew the expression on Hart's face. She was chewing the inside of her lip in thought. If she could, she would have gnawed at her fingers, but that was an unpleasant prospect considering their current occupation.

Edmond watched as she took a fork she had found in the kitchen and patiently scraped the clotted blood away from the girl's brain matter, depositing it as neatly as possible in a tupperware container.

"This is what killed her," Hart said. Edmond shot her a wry look. He likely could have figured that out even without the aid of an instructional Internet video. Hart didn't seem to notice. "But this shouldn't have happened to her."

She had a point. Bots were hardly designed to be prone to massive brain bleeding. Edmond himself had spent years perfecting the Bots, designing a biological system free from all the usual failings of the human body. A Bot should never get cancer, heart disease, even the common cold. A Bot definitely shouldn't have an aneurism.

"Maybe someone hit her?" Edmond offered.

"Or she fell." While the Bots were protected from most human illnesses, he had made sure that they could experience physical trauma. Though he had expected that feature would be jettisoned as soon as the Army started producing their own units.

Hart shook her head. "I checked her body. The only sign of trauma is a small abrasion on the skin at the temple." She turned the half-skull on its side to show Edmond. The skin, still intact, was marred by a rashy red line. It didn't look deadly.

Edmond glanced down at the rest of the girl's body. Hart had peeled off her clothes before covering her respectfully in a worn flannel sheet. The skin that Edmond could see was unblemished, though it did have a slightly waxy texture, a golden cast that signaled to everyone that she was no longer alive.

The girl's brain was an odd, pinkish-brownish color, like well-chewed gum. Hart touched it with her bare fingers, manipulating the brain this way and that, looking for anything unusual. "It's . . . bigger . . . I think. Bigger than it should be, probably swollen from all the pressure."

She picked up her X-acto knife, pushing the brain to one side of the skull with her free hand. Hart inserted the blade and began patiently slicing away at something underneath the brain. Likely the midbrain, where the brain connected with the central nervous system.

For the first time, Edmond noticed that Hart had tied her hair back with an elastic band that she must have found somewhere inside the cabin. It struck him, as those tiny moments of human practicality always did when it came to Hart. He wondered uselessly what she thought about her hair, about its growth, about the way it fell silken over her forehead and eyes.

Hart released a shaky breath that pulled Edmond

from his musings. Slowly, as though she expected it to explode in her hands, she lifted the brain out of the dead girl's skull and placed it in the largest plastic container. Almost immediately, a shallow puddle of clear fluid formed around it in the bottom of the container.

"This." For a fraction of a second, she smiled. But it was, after all, a dead child stretched out before her. Her face did not so much fall as relax into a look of grim blankness. She pointed the tip of the X-acto knife at a strange growth on the right side of the child's empty skull. It looked like an un-inflated balloon, hugging the wall of her head.

"Blood clot?" Edmond asked. The strange, bag-like structure was red and appeared to be mottled with darker blue and purple veins.

Hart frowned and shook her head. Using her blade, she scraped the strange thing away from the skull and lifted it up to the fluorescent kitchen lights to examine it. Red stained her fingers.

"This is synthetic," she said. "They made this and then they put it inside of her head."

And, all at once, Edmond realized exactly what had happened. The Army had introduced "improvements" to his design after all. He supposed it made a certain kind of sense. Having a device that allowed the controllers to remotely shut down a Bot would have solved a lot of the Army's problems. And they must be having problems if scrapping an entire otherwise functional unit was the preferable option. SennTech must have piggybacked on this new, morbid tech the way they had piggybacked on every other part of the Bot design.

It seemed that Hart too had realized what the strange object was doing there in the little girl's head. The corners of her mouth had turned down so resolutely, if the situation had been less serious, it might have made Edmond laugh. She looked very much like a child trying desperately not to burst into tears. Her jaw quivered slightly, as though suffering under a great effort.

"We should bury her," Hart said gently. The silence had become a thing that might break and she handled it as carefully as she had handled every part of the girl's body. "That is what people do with their dead."

"I . . . I don't know about that," Edmond said hesitantly. He put a hand on her bare forearm so she would know that he was not against her, that he meant her every comfort. "The ground will be very hard right now because of the cold and . . . " he glanced down at the dead girl. Her eyes were still open because Hart had not seen fit to close them. They were vacant and beginning to cloud over. Edmond was suddenly reminded of the fact that the girl was not long dead at all. Less than two hours ago, she had been alive and upright and talking to them.

"And," he continued, "I'm not sure we want to bury evidence like this. Someone might find it."

Hart nodded slowly. "You're right," she said. "She is evidence and they would want her back."

As though she had heard him, or heard his thoughts, Hart reached out and pressed a single finger to the girl's right eyelid, she slid it down with a painful solemnity before doing the same thing to the other eye.

They stood together in silence. Edmond wondered what, if anything, he should be thinking. If he were the praying sort, he might have said something for . . . for her soul? Edmond wasn't sure if that was a concept he necessarily believed in. He had built Hart, after all, from the ground up, and he had not, at any point in the process, inserted a soul. Nevertheless, there was something undeniably human in her and in this little girl as well.

In the end, Edmond settled for hoping that the bloody, internal explosion that had killed her was not too painful. He also hoped that the life before it had not been too hard. He knew, at the very least, that it was not very long. SennTech was light years away from building something this advanced when Edmond and Hart had escaped. Something big must have changed since then and fairly recently as well. Edmond couldn't imagine that they would just sit on a potential cash cow like this girl for very long.

"I'm going to gather some things," Hart said. "Do you think you could find more wood?"

---○---

The first thing that Edmond thought of was Snow White in her glass coffin.

True, the makeshift pyre that Hart had assembled outside the cabin on the shores of the frozen lake was not made of glass, and the girl on top of it was hardly a fairytale princess, but there was something to the ritual of it all. It felt old and strangely enchanted.

He had scraped together all the loose wood he could find, even venturing out into the forest and grabbing fallen branches from the ground. He pulled some sticks and twigs off the trees as best he could and deposited them in the little circle where Hart had cleared away the snow. She spent the better part of the afternoon building the pyre, a thick bed to support the girl's body with a half-canopy of thinner, more flexible branches to arch over her head.

No flowers grew here in the dead of winter, so Hart deconstructed a dusty old wreath full of plastic and cloth flowers, weaving them in amongst the branches. A wicker basket from the bathroom full of desiccated potpourri was patiently spread over the girl's body. All of it had the earnest but improvisational feeling of a child's imaginary game.

"These are your death customs, aren't they?" she asked him once. Her whole face was like an open wound, impossibly vulnerable.

"Not mine, personally," Edmond said. "But yes. This is what people do. To pay their respects."

As for the girl herself, Hart had put her back

together as well as she could and re-dressed her. She carried her out to the pyre in two pieces, lying her body down first and then balancing her severed skull carefully in, more or less, its original position. She laid the girl's arms down by her sides and brushed out her hair with her fingers. She sprayed the girl's throat and chest with a nearly-empty glass bottle of perfume she had found in one of the bathrooms. It smelled like someone's grandmother.

Finally, Hart produced a small fabric doll and laid it beside the girl. The doll was in the Raggedy Ann mold with black yarn hair and button eyes. She wore a red apron and had little brown boots sewed on. It was a bit juvenile for someone of the girl's age, Edmond thought, but he knew that Hart was trying her very best, so he said nothing.

They lit the pyre in several places so it would be sure to catch. They shielded the little infant flames with their bodies until the fire began. It rose higher and hotter while Hart and Edmond watched, circling around the pyre as the wind changed and sent ash fluttering towards them.

The smell was horrible. Meat charring but also rot and the eerie, musty smell of old, wet wood in conflagration. Hart did not seem to notice the scent, however, and she just stood there with her arms crossed over her chest.

"You watch until it's done," she said once, quietly. "That is how you give respect."

In all their travels, Edmond and Hart had, naturally, become quite physically close. On the pot farm, they had slept side-by-side in thin sleeping bags on the floors, next to an ever-rotating roster of workers. In the truck, of course, they were crammed into a few scant feet of space. They had camped once in a while, stretching their legs flat in the truck's bed or on the hard ground. Yet in all that time, they had never once shared a bed with one another.

Partially, it was due to Hart's aversion to sleep. She had no particular need for it and instead chose to spend her time completing any work left undone during the day. When they were on the road, she occupied herself with mysterious tasks while Edmond slept. Once or twice, he had seen her ferreting away a notebook as he woke up. He had asked her not to leave the truck while he slept but sometimes, when he awoke briefly in the night, he had a blind, unthinking feeling that she was very far away from him.

When the pyre had burned down, leaving the bones of the girl behind, Edmond had staggered into the cabin. His fingers were numb, though he'd been wearing a huge pair of wool mittens over the thin, synthetic gloves he already owned. His face, nevertheless, was red and radiant from the fire's heat. He peeled off his endless layers stiffly and painfully.

Hart followed him, standing in the miniature kitchen looking like a ghost. The moon was two-thirds full and it poured light in through the windows. Her eyes, the side of her face, her hair, all was luminous.

Years ago, on a late-night trip home from a robotics competition, he had pointed at a full, orange moon out the window of the teacher's minivan. Kelsey P. had chided them, telling him that the moon was a lady and one should never point at a lady.

"It's bad luck," she had said, grabbing his hand and pulling it down.

He had chuckled at her—he had always been told that there was a man in the moon, canny and winking, like a jovial uncle.

But now, looking at Hart, his first thought was, *She is like the moon.* Remote and blue and so incredibly lovely. She seemed close, so close he might have reached out and touched her. But in reality, she was in another world, a near-immeasurable distance away from him.

"I have to sleep," he told her gently. "If you like, you can fiddle with the radio. I think we should be able to get it working pretty easily."

Hart didn't say anything. She didn't move. Her face was half in shadow and Edmond couldn't make out her eyes. It suddenly seemed important that he see her expression.

But he did not move and she did not move.

After a moment, Edmond turned and walked towards the single bedroom at the back of the cabin. He heard a delicate shuffling behind him, the creak of old floorboards, but he didn't look back.

What was that old story? That myth about the man who descends into hell for the woman he loves and he can lead her out again, but only if he never, never looks behind him? And, of course, he cannot resist. He looks and he watches her vanish . . .

Edmond did not look behind him.

In the bedroom, it was much darker. Curtains drawn across the windows blocked out the strange, blue moonlight almost entirely. Edmond felt his way over to the bed and crawled into it, peeling back the blankets and sheets which hadn't been used or aired out in years, apparently.

The linens smelled clean but old, like the pages of an antique book. The sheets were cool against Edmonds hands and arms. He felt the bed depress slightly as Hart sat down. For a moment, she simply sat there, as though she were tucking him in.

Eventually, however, Hart laid down. It was less a voluntary motion than a short-distance fall. She remained fully clothed, even her shoes were still on and she curled up on top of the blankets.

Edmond wondered if she was crying.

"I want to sleep," she said, her voice sounded whispery and brittle. "I want to not see anything or hear anything or feel anything."

Edmond nodded and then, realizing she couldn't see him, said, "I can help you."

He sat up, covers spilling around him, and

took her by the shoulders. She was unresisting, doll-like, as he removed her large coat, her man's sweater, her flannel button-down. He untied her shoes and deposited them in a tumble beside the bed. He undid the button on her jeans and she helped him shimmy them off. Underneath, she wore a black and nubbly pair of long johns. It was a kind of costume she wore, Human Woman Disguise. In reality, Hart provided her own heat and light and did not suffer from the frailties of Edmond's kind.

She trembled and, if Edmond had not known of her superior resistance to temperature extremes, he might have imagined she was, in that moment, experiencing cold.

He opened the covers to her, the space underneath now somewhat warmed by his body heat. She fit herself against his body and he wrapped his arms around her midsection, burying his face in her hair, which smelled of ash and death.

"Close your eyes," he said softly. "Close your eyes

and pay attention to your breathing. It will happen so quietly and so slowly, you won't even know."

Hart breathed deeply through her nose, like a diver preparing to leap into a freezing pool. Edmond tightened his arms around her and she seemed to flow into the negative space that his body made. She rested there, breathing loose and easy.

Together, they slept.

SEVEN
THE LOST DOG

London, United Kingdom. September, 2045

It was in London and it was so stupid, what finally happened to Ebert.

Movement became very difficult in the days following his flight from Brussels. As he had expected, video and images of Avon on the floor of the café had quickly spread across all corners of the Internet.

"Public freakouts" as the video was most often tagged, were a dime-a-dozen. It was the end of the video, however, when Avon had used a jagged shard of broken plate to cut his face, pulling the skin away from his skull with no apparent signs of pain.

Avon had shouted, semi-coherently, about Bots,

about his assignment. About a young couple, a girl and a boy. They were dead. From the way Avon spoke about them (screamed about them), it was his fault. Or maybe he only wished it had been his fault? It was difficult to make out much of anything from the videos.

A number of self-appointed investigators had aggressively pursued the videos and the story behind it, leading more legitimate news sources to take up the cause. From there, things had snowballed quickly. Some clever journalist sniffed out a money trail and started hounding the weapons division of the Army for details on what everyone was calling "super STs."

Ebert didn't like the name. After all, Hart Series' Bots were their creator, Edmond West's original goal. They were always the intention. The SennTech Bots were a poor and venal sidetrack into corporate interest.

It was largely as Sheba had predicted. The military, backed into a corner, sent their smiling, matronly PR flak to explain the "experimental, first stages, Bot program" that had produced Avon and a handful of others like him. They spun it as a major advancement in artificial intelligence but, like any other major innovation, there would be "bumps in the road."

Ebert was obsessed with these reports. Whenever he had reliable Internet access and a moment to himself, he was searching any combination of key words that might lead him to more information on how the Army was tackling this problem.

It was clear to him that the first issue the military had to deal with was the perception of Bots as weapons. Profoundly dangerous weapons that were apparently "loose" as a result of the Army's policies. Many of the interviews had been hitting the safety issue hard. Again and again, they were flogging the idea of some "new, cutting-edge modifications" that had effectively neutered the Bots. They underscored the idea that these Bots were few in number: "You have a better chance of being killed by a falling coconut than by a SuperST," the PR flak said again and again, a little hidden chortle in her voice.

Try though he did, however, Ebert couldn't find any specific references to what these new modifications might actually be.

He also hadn't been able to find any actual concrete information on what had happened to Avon. Most of the videos cut out before he left the coffee shop. If, indeed, that was what happened. There were some alleged eyewitness reports available online, but they all contradicted one another. Avon was injected with something by men in American military uniforms and dragged out. Avon smashed a window and ran out into the street. Avon was shot multiple times. Avon was forced into a private taxicab. There was no way of knowing which—if any—of these possibilities was the truth.

Soon, other blogs started cropping up to refute the first ones. Avon was just a crazy guy. It was a viral video stunt for a new TV show. It was some makeup artist trying to get attention for their work.

He was fixated on Avon at least in part because the other Bots had almost certainly been abducted. He was still in a full communications blackout with every other Bot he knew and he had no idea where any one of them might be. Avon, though, Avon could only be a handful of places, none of them good.

Ebert sometimes told himself that he had done his best for Avon and that, given the situation, staying would have been the worst possible course of action. He couldn't help Avon in the midst of his . . . episode. They would have been taken together. Sometimes, he even suggested to himself that Avon would have wanted him to escape, but he had no real reason for believing that. Avon had never said anything like that and speculating about his motives was a useless exercise.

But, most of the time, Ebert didn't tell himself anything at all. He simply scrolled through page after page of results, peered uselessly at low-resolution videos, attempted to parse the meaning behind tortured publicity-speak.

For the most part, he accessed the Internet in libraries or in one of the vanishingly rare Internet cafés that still existed. Ebert didn't dare try to get work or otherwise engage with mainstream society. The cash he had on him when he left Brussels would have to get him where he was going.

And he had no idea where that was.

At the moment, he was living in a little tent city within sight of the train tracks. The others there—backpackers, homeless, street punks and anyone else who had nowhere else to go—all said that the camp was bound to be "liquidated" soon enough. Those places usually didn't last past a few weeks, everyone said. Ebert didn't know what he would do when the encampment was gone. Possibly move on altogether.

There was a voice in his head that whispered to him about how unsustainable all this was. London or Sao Paulo or Taipei, no matter where he went, he would essentially be living under the same cloud. And it seemed that every day it dropped lower and lower, crushing him underneath.

There was no future without a network. He had to regroup and find the other Bots, if any of them remained. One person, alone, had so little power. And, each day, Ebert felt more and more exhausted. He had thought it was difficult in Brussels, living all the time with the sensation of being watched, but it was infinitely worse now. He lacked even the luxury of a private space, relatively safe, where he could be anxious by himself.

It was no wonder that, in this position of weakness, alone in a vacuum of information, his enemies found it very easy to capture him.

It was an older protocol, from before Brussels even. That should have tipped Ebert off right away, but he wanted to believe that someone had wriggled through the net and made it to him. A lost-dog flyer was posted around town, a Pekingese-pug mix with a mean, lopsided little face and a dramatic overbite. It was astonishingly ugly, designed to be noticed.

This was a photo they had agreed upon, specifically for its unusual properties. He found it water damaged, despite a plastic sheath, pinned to a news board outside the university. He tore it from the board and, in a nearly involuntary motion, pressed it to his chest like a long-lost family member.

Below the picture, there were a series of numbers. First a contact phone number, then an address. Ebert mentally stripped away the letters, leaving only the numbers behind: 51541327014639011740. Coordinates for a proposed meeting and a time: Thursdays at 5:40 p.m.

It was exactly as they had planned months and months ago. The idea was that one Bot would paper neighborhoods with such flyers as soon as they set up in a new city. Other Bots would keep an eye out for them and respond if they located one. Ebert had tacitly dissolved this practice when they fled Brussels, because he feared that the things which made it stand out to a roaming Bot would also draw the attention of other parties.

But if someone had never come to Brussels, had never learned of the prohibition of this particular tactic, they might well know nothing of the overall situation. They might be sitting ducks. More importantly, they might be someone that Ebert could trust. It would be very good to trust someone again, to allow himself to rest, if only for a moment.

The coordinates led him to Camden Town, to the locks on Regent's Canal. The adjacent market occupied revamped and repurposed industrial buildings. There were many chambers inside the market and tight little walkways between the innumerable vendors. It seemed constantly bursting with visitors, many of them apparently tourists. Ebert wove between the sellers and the buyers, passing tables full of costume jewelry, artfully ripped bags, and pants studded with glinting metal.

Ebert had a method for vetting newly arrived Bots. It was unscientific but, thus far, it had not led him astray. Whenever he was meeting a new potential Bot, he paid very close attention to that vague but insistent feeling of *known-ness*, as though he were encountering some element of his distant childhood. There was no good reason that Ebert should be able to "sense" a Bot, and yet he had always been able to, from the earliest days after his activation.

And so now he moved purposefully through the crowd, paying keen attention to the people around him. Who appeared to be waiting, who appeared bored, who appeared uninterested in the wares on display. Who felt like a fellow Bot.

There was a girl standing next to the entrance, half-hidden behind the door to block out the wind.

She was young and very tall. She had a short, brownish-gold afro. It looked not unlike a halo.

She stared out into the night beyond the door. She hid from the wind, but did not seem especially cold in her coat, which came down to her calves, but was of thin material. It was more of a raincoat than a winter coat.

It was 5:37. Edmond didn't know how long she habitually waited for anyone to meet with her, but he wanted to observe her a little while longer before he made contact. As he watched, she did not look away from the open door, though she fiddled with something in her pocket. She seemed slightly keyed up, though Ebert supposed that was normal for someone about to potentially have a clandestine meeting.

Ebert knew that there was a chance that this was some sort of trap. He supposed there must be plenty of Bots, fully functional, fully obedient, that would have no problem finding and recapturing others just like themselves. But he would not be able to decide if she were that sort of Bot or not simply by watching her stand in the cold. If he waited too long, she would surely leave and then he would have to wait another week. Plus, she could, at any time, decide that the protocol was too dangerous or ineffective and quit showing up.

It was a risk, but that risk extended in both directions.

He didn't know if it was weakness or pragmatism, but at 5:57 he went to her and touched her shoulder.

She did not smile, as he might have expected. Instead of looking relieved or excited, she seemed surprised. For all her staring out into the street, she apparently hadn't really expected anyone to come.

"Hello," Ebert said. "My name is Ebert. Do you . . . have a name?"

Her eyes widened slightly. "I . . . uh . . . no. No name yet."

Suddenly, Ebert found himself uncertain. There was nothing about her specifically that might invite this feeling. She certainly had that ineffable something that always signaled to Ebert that he was in the presence of someone like himself. And yet he had a misgiving, as though he had made some horrible mistake.

"Did you . . . lose your dog?" he asked her.

"Oh yes, yes," she said quickly. "That was me. With the ad."

Ebert smiled. It felt shaky, even to him. "Good," he said. "I'm glad. I'm so glad you're here."

Again, there was the absence of her smile.

"Come outside, we can talk." She led him to a small courtyard created by the structure of locks. A number of picnic-style tables were set up there and groups of people were laughing and drinking and eating. Electric lights were looped overhead. They had just started to glow in the late spring gloaming.

The nameless woman sat him down at a table in the far corner. It was not under any lights and a nearby wall cast it mostly in shadows.

"How long have you been here?" Ebert asked

in a low voice. Nothing they were saying would necessarily alert an observer to their presence, but still his feeling of ready paranoia lingered.

"Not long." She seemed uneasy. Her eyes flickered all around them and never came to rest on Ebert's face. She, too, must be worried about being watched.

"Are there others?" he asked. She shook her head solemnly.

"I was in Brussels," Ebert said. The woman's eyes widened.

"With the . . . ?"

"Yeah," Ebert said gently. "He was . . . my friend." Friend was perhaps not the correct word. The relationship that Bots had to one another was not cleanly mapped on to any existing dynamic that Ebert knew of. There was something familial to it but also an element of estrangement. It was frequently hard for him to know whether or not he was fond of a particular Bot or simply felt a visceral need to protect and cherish them as part of a small—and dwindling—population.

Perhaps Avon had not been his friend, but he had felt responsible for him. Avon, who was fragile, was owed more than the average Bot. To call him a friend, a brother, allowed Ebert to inch closer to honesty about what had happened in that café. Only one kind of person leaves a friend behind to a certainly awful fate.

"I'm sorry," the nameless woman said and she sounded very sincere. Which was why it surprised Ebert so much when she reached out and pressed a small, TASER-like device against the side of his neck. He didn't have much time to feel surprised, however, before two vampiric prongs shot out of the device and into his skin. Something pulsed in his neck and then there was a rich and comforting blackness and then nothing at all.

When he awoke, Ebert had a moment of pure ease—he could be anywhere, anything might happen next. He hoped that it had been the same way for Avon. A single pulse and then nothingness. Avon loved to sleep, perhaps it had felt like sleeping to him.

Ebert, however, had to wake up.

It was actually the smell of the place that he recognized first. A sterility, the sweet, sharp odor of a certain kind of cleaning product that the lab always used. There was another scent as well, closer and more . . . human.

He knew her perfume, wheat-y and floral, an odd concession to femininity from someone so carefully professional. The lab director, Dr. Barber-Neal leaned over him, a tiny flashlight in one hand.

"Follow the light," she said, upon realizing he was awake. "Just your eyes, not your head."

Ebert did as he was asked. Dr. Barber-Neal's voice was one of the first he had ever heard upon activation. All his life, she had ordered and he had complied. If he did so now, in his disorientation, he could be forgiven because habits do die hard.

"Good," she murmured before ticking off something on a flex-tablet. Ebert was lying down on a silver table of the sort used to move dead bodies. He was suddenly aware of the uncomfortable hardness of the metal, the way his head just flopped loose and unsupported. They might have put him on a gurney instead of hauling him around like a slab of butchered meat.

"How are you feeling, HS C-27699?" she asked him, smiling benevolently. Ebert swallowed hard, his throat was thick and his tongue tasted foul. He wondered how long he had been . . . gone.

That was the only way he could describe it. He had never experienced anything like that. He wondered if it was a feeling like death. Temporary death.

"What did she do to me?" His voice pushed out of his sticky throat, becoming almost a whistle.

"Electromagnetic pulse," Dr. Barber-Neal said.

"It induces a brief . . . " she paused, as though carefully selecting her words, "system overload."

"How brief?" Ebert swallowed again. His voice was starting to return.

"You were in blackout for 94 hours."

94 hours. *Fuck.*

"All systems are online now," Dr. Barber-Neal offered, completely misinterpreting Ebert's alarmed expression. "And we haven't seen any lasting damage with this technique. You should be fine."

And then Dr. Barber-Neal did a very strange thing. She reached down and found Ebert's limp hand. She squeezed it once in a familiar sort of way. Her face was uncertain and she dropped his hand almost immediately, but the touch remained, like a half-hearted apology.

"What's going to happen to me?" Ebert whispered, he turned his face towards her even as she looked away, fiddling with her flex-tablet and tucking her chin into her collar to hide her expression.

"It's just a simple modification. An upgrade, in

many ways," she said. Her voice sounded very far away and suddenly she was so different from the woman who had, just moments before, taken his hand for no reason other than simple pity.

Before Ebert had the chance to ask more questions, there came a discordant metallic sound from the hallway outside the laboratory. Dr. Barber-Neal ran over to the door, peering out through the little viewing window.

"Shit!" she said, throwing open the door and rushing out. As the door swung closed, Ebert saw Dr. Barber-Neal and Dr. Kim struggling with another person. A Bot, he suspected, though how could he be sure? The Bot was a young man, he looked like a teenager, with long black hair. He was resisting them and fairly effectively, it seemed.

And the door swung back on its hinges, like a curtain falling on a stage play. Slowly, Ebert sat up on his mortuary table. Shapes moved in the window and there was the occasional sounds of something heavy slamming into a cement wall or a tiled floor.

Eventually, Dr. Barber-Neal and Dr. Kim burst back in through the door. Dr. Kim's face had turned an alarming shade of crimson and her loose ponytail hung sideways on her head.

"That's the fourth non-military HS we've found!" she said, her voice rising to a hysterical pitch. "Where are these things coming from?"

Dr. Barber-Neal, far more collected, said only, "Can we really call them Hart Series, considering?"

Dr. Kim let out a huff. "What are we supposed to do with them?"

"The same thing we would do with any other wayward unit."

Dr. Kim looked over at Ebert, apparently noticing him for the first time. "Ah." She said. "HS C-27699."

"Dr. Kim," Ebert said weakly.

She turned back to the older woman and inclined her head until the two of them were in a kind of awkward huddle. Nevertheless, Ebert heard her when she asked, "Should we be discussing this in front of him?"

"He's scheduled for surgery in twenty-four minutes," Dr. Barber-Neal said, at normal volume. "It's fine."

Dr. Kim looked at him as though she weren't exactly sure.

"So we're going to modify all of them? Even—" she gestured out towards the hallway. Dr. Barber-Neal nodded. Dr. Kim folded her arms as though she were cold. "I don't know, Janelle. What if we get in there and find some nasty surprise? We don't know anything about their composition or their creator. They could be . . . booby trapped. "

Dr. Barber-Neal smiled at her. "That's not exactly true." She gave the younger woman a meaningful look. "We know exactly who is producing these things and, if I know Edmond West at all, he would not integrate anything into a Bot that might harm it. So. No booby traps." After a moment of silence, Dr. Barber-Neal clapped her hands and turned towards Ebert.

"Now," she said briskly, "let's get you prepped for surgery, shall we?"

She walked over to the table, where Ebert was still sitting, bewildered. There was a part of him that seriously considered leaping off the table and hurling it at the women, running out that door and . . . then what?

That door would be followed by dozens just like it. He didn't have the access codes and he didn't have any compatriots. He would be caught, probably stabbed with that vile EMP thing again and wind up right back here, on this table, waiting to be modified along with all the rest of the others, the ones he hadn't saved and the ones he hadn't even met yet.

He tried not to think, most of the time, about how fragile humans were when compared to his own physical body. But as he looked up into Dr. Barber-Neal's smiling face, he could not help but think about how, with the right application of force, he could grab her lower jaw and rip it cleanly away from her face.

He could kill them, these doctors. But he could not kill all the doctors between himself and freedom. He could not kill a whole world of humans. He had been designed to think strategically and to find the best course of action in any given situation. And so he sat still and waited.

Dr. Barber-Neal touched his hair fondly, ruffling it like a big sister. "It'll be a shame to shave this off," she said. "But it'll grow back." And then, her voice very different, her eyes very soft, Dr. Barber-Neal said to him, "Don't worry. Everything will be okay."

EIGHT

ISLAND TIME

ISLA REDONDA, MEXICO. NOVEMBER, 2045

Washington, Michigan, Ontario, North-west Territories, Alaska . . . eventually, they went so far north that they were forced to move south.

The island had a bad reputation amongst the mainlanders. It occupied an uneasy territory sand-wiched between Mexico and Guatemala out in the North Pacific. Some people had told them that the US government used to do atomic testing out there, but Edmond found that unlikely. Other people were more straightforward, saying that it had been a plague island and was now haunted by the ghosts of the sickly dead. Still others said there was an unnamed "something" that lived out there, a creature not yet known to science who consumed any wayward travelers. The most practical said that the island was simply a dumping ground, a place where people put their trash, old appliances, even the occasional dead body in need of concealment.

Sometimes, glittering, multi-colored sea glass washed up on the mainland shore and people said it was bottle remnants from all the discarded trash.

Edmond liked the island because it was difficult to access. There were no chartered tourist boats out there, it wasn't particularly close to any other, more popular islands. The best boat launch to get to the island was in a half-hidden cove on a particularly rocky shore. And if one did manage to find the boat launch and get down to the shore (there was only a little footpath leading down two-hundred fifty feet of rocky cliff), they could only launch during the forty-seven minute interval when the tides would actually allow a vessel to make landfall on the island.

In terms of remoteness, it was by far the best of their many refuges.

For all these reasons, they had, more or less, made the island their home for the last two months.

The island was nine miles around and it came roughly to a point in the center. There was abundant plant life, but much of it was either useless or actively hostile to humans. There were some odd remains here and there, half-buried structures made of concrete with pointed rebar bones sticking out willy-nilly and big pits of poorly-concealed garbage. There weren't many animals, at least not ones that Edmond saw, though he did frequently hear odd chitters and shrieks in the night.

Perhaps that was only the plague ghosts.

The biggest problem was that of supplies and Edmond had left it in Hart's capable hands. Somehow, she had secured a monthly air drop of various necessities, mainly for Edmond. Hart, after all, could live indefinitely, even in this place so inimical to human habitation.

They made for themselves a makeshift home in the shell of some sort of storage facility. There were many chambers, all of them made of cement, and some of them even had a roof overhead. Most, however, just had enormous craters that let the night sky pour in.

It was rarely cold. Edmond slept often, night or day. His skin moved through an endless cycle of burn, peel, burn again. He never had been one to tan. Hart's skin, synthetic though it was, transformed. Under the beating sun, she turned a fine, reddish gold color, like someone had dipped her in discreet blusher.

Her hair grew so long. On those rare occasions when she deigned to sleep beside him, it got everywhere. It covered his face like a thin veil made of coarse netting. It clung to his mouth, tangled in his eyelashes and when she left, it was a palpable presence wherever she had been. Long, dark brown hair stood out against their pale linens like exclamation marks. She left her little reminders everywhere.

It was on one of those nights when, for the first time, Edmond thought seriously about sex. Sex with Hart.

At some point, he had somehow established a thin and permeable barrier to such ideas in his mind. Whenever such ideas threatened to rear their heads, he would think back upon Hart's earliest days, upon her asking him what they were to one another. Brother? Father? God? How could he add more to that? The weight would surely send the two of them toppling.

And so he said nothing.

But he wondered if Hart thought about it as well.

Thus far, she had showed little to no interest in human sexuality, though he was sure she knew how the . . . mechanics worked. She was very well-read. She had never questioned him about it, though, and that was very strange for Hart, whose curiosity was boundless and exhausting.

And what could he have told her if she did ask? He knew all of the things that she could probably read about online, the definitions and the physiology. But what could he tell her of experience? He himself had not been with a woman in a long time. Once, the night after graduation, with Kelsey P. The two of them had fallen into one another more than anything else. It was the Senior All-Nite Party and there was some sense in the air that Edmond was about to fly away and never return. Kelsey had taken him out to the edge of the track field and his virginity had evaporated into the night air.

Since then, lovers were few and far between. One girl in college, and most of what he remembered was the taste of silver tequila and yellow bile. Twice, the same woman when he was working at the lab. She lived in his apartment building and had a cat that was always escaping. "I think you're a really nice guy," she used to tell him, as though he had ever asked her opinion on the matter.

Not for the first time, Edmond was acutely aware of the irony inherent in the idea of anyone learning to be human from him. Of course, Hart had taken her own path to humanity and had produced something quite unlike Edmond. Quite unlike anyone else at all.

Sometimes, on those nights when he was allowed to wrap his arms around her, he would touch the skin on her stomach, the soft place just below her belly button.

I made that he could not help but think. *I built that in my lab. I spent weeks designing this skin, this flesh.*

"There's a myth," she whispered to him one night. She was facing away from him. Her hair picked up the moonlight and sent it back, eerie and blue. "That human beings shed their cells in a predictable fashion so that every seven years, they are an entirely new person."

Was she thinking then about her own flesh? Her cells, birthed and sloughed off as constantly as any ordinary woman's? In seven years' time, perhaps she would no longer be the woman he had made. She would be entirely new, a snake that shed its skin. She would leave her Bot-skin behind, a ghost or a photo negative of the woman she used to be.

Sometimes, without really meaning to, Edmond would kiss her hair. It was, he told himself, a consequence of their proximity. His face against her skull, there was nowhere else to go. Her hair flooded him, drenched him. Her hair kissed every part of him and so he kissed this smallest part of her.

———o———

A few things had made the trip from Michigan

all the way to the island. Perhaps the most important of them was the old hand-crank radio, which was their best way of keeping on top of the global Bot situation. It had become ever more dire in the last few months.

The radio had informed them about the launch of the "kill-switch-enabled Hart Series." The safest AI on the military market, though it was hardly approved for commercial use. The radio had carried reports of demonstrations, Bots disobeying direct orders and then falling helplessly to the ground as though felled by an outraged god.

Obviously, there was no visual on the radio, but Edmond and Hart didn't need a visual. Edmond saw, again and again, the little girl behind the counter bleeding and falling. The look of terrible knowing in her eyes.

Every kill-switch-enabled Bot was acutely aware of the time bomb inside their heads. That was, as the military said, the beauty of the program. "The Bot has become a self-policing machine,"

Andrea Davos-San Miguel said. They had learned to recognize her voice, the Army's chief public relations officer. "Kill switch technology is centered around a very simple truth: no organism is going to act contrary to its own survival. Safety is often a matter of finding very simple solutions."

Sometimes, the radio also brought them news of themselves. Or rather, of Edmond. No one ever mentioned Hart herself and in fact the PR flacks took great care to avoid even saying "Hart Series" preferring the HS abbreviation and declining to indicate what, exactly it stood for.

Still, Edmond was their great bogeyman. A convenient explanation for the dissemination of Bots who acted contrary to the "simple solution" of the kill switch. Bots who attacked humans, Bots who destroyed other Bots, Bots who did not disclose their Bot status and were later discovered burrowed deeply into human life, like a monstrous tick.

Those Bots, the Army claimed, were coming

directly from disgraced roboticist Edmond West, the unhinged fanatic who was currently evading capture. According to the radio, Edmond was obsessed with designing a "superior being" who would overcome and, eventually, supplant debauched humanity.

The Edmond West on the radio was deeply mentally ill and fixated on the idea of a utopian world where only Bots existed. "We are pursuing him with the full force of the US military," the radio promised.

Of course, it was fiction. The "Westian" Bots, uncontrolled by kill switch technology were probably just remnants of an earlier generation of the Hart Series. Or, it was possible that they were, in fact, kill-switch-ennabled and the machines occasionally did choose to act contrary to their own self-interest, despite what the Army thought about "self-preservation."

If Edmond had learned anything at all from all of this, it was that Bots could be counted upon to mirror all the irregularities and perversions of human behavior. Whatever it was that drove humans to jump off bridges or blow themselves up or leap in front of a bullet meant for another, it existed in Bots as well.

Hart listened to the radio broadcasts with an eerie stillness. It was as though she were holding on tightly to herself, lest she fly apart into a thousand different pieces. Edmond knew of her anger in an intellectual sense, but he could not, himself, feel it.

And Hart, of course, gave no windows or doors into her heart. Ever since that night in the lab, when they had driven all through the night, when Edmond had poured his own blood into her, she had become so closed and circumspect. Where once it had seemed as though the whole world passed through her and was absorbed, now she seemed so hesitant, so shuttered.

After a particularly awful broadcast, she would vanish. Edmond had an idea that she went up to the top of the island. She kept some kind of sanctuary there, a place where she could be utterly alone. Out of respect, Edmond never followed her.

It might be hours or it might be days, but she would always return to him.

The man who brought their supplies was called Jeb. He was from Texas, originally. His hair was silvery and short and he almost always wore small, perfectly round sunglasses. He was very fond of Hart and he deferred to her like an old-fashioned gentleman.

Edmond had never asked Hart how she had contacted him. Likely she had used her makeshift computer, which she had also carted along on their travels. She swore to him that she accessed the North American wi-fi network only sparingly and always behind multiple proxies, but Edmond still didn't like the idea. Edmond had a suspicion that Hart was in contact with other Bots, at least to some degree, and he figured that Jeb was someone else with pro-Bot leanings whom she had met online.

Sometimes it struck him how absurd their lives had quickly become. "Pro-Bot leanings." As soon as the Army broadcast the existence of Hart Series Bots, people had begun to pick sides. Each day, the factions proliferated. Those who saw Bots as a herald of the end times, a species sure to wipe humans off the face of the earth, or the smaller but distinct subset that saw the Bots as a terrible example of American supremacy, the H-bomb of the AI age. Then there were those who approached Bots as a distinct, sapient life form to be engaged with on equal footing with humans.

And, of course, the largest population was that of consumers who wanted Bots of their very own. According to the radio, SennTech had already announced plans to roll out a series of HS Bots for private citizens. "We meet every need." Nothing was mentioned of an earlier wave of such creatures. Nothing was mentioned of a little dead girl.

Edmond tried not to dwell on his role in all of this—though it was, on occasion, unavoidable. He could not deny that he had toppled the first domino and everything that had come to pass was a result of his decades of dedicated work. Sometimes, when he thought about those years, he found himself unable to recognize himself in the choices he had made.

Who was that man who loved creation so much? Who was so single minded and so firmly convinced of his own rightness?

These days, Edmond wasn't convinced of anything at all. All of his decisions seemed flawed and when he reflected upon them, he could only see the places where he had failed. Even his flight from the lab now seemed a woefully naive move. He had hoped that, by taking Hart and attempting to destroy all of his notes, he might have stymied the Army's attempts to recreate his discoveries.

He should have known that nothing he did at the laboratory was private, nothing was safe. If he had thought further, he might have stayed. At the lab he would have had the opportunity to exercise some degree of control over his work. Perhaps it would have been better to work within the system after all. At the very least, he wouldn't have the entire US armed forces trying to find and, likely, murder him.

Most of all, he regretted what his decisions meant for Hart. He wanted a better life for her. Or even just a life. Something simple, granted to every other human on the planet. He thought that couldn't happen behind laboratory walls, but maybe he would have been able to protect her there.

In the lab, she would not have been fondled by a room full of men with medals on their chests. She would not have been shot. She would not have watched that girl die. She would have been, for lack of a better word, safe.

Edmond thought sometimes about apologizing to her, but he knew that if he began to tell Hart how sorry he was, he would never, ever stop. It would come pouring out of him, his grief and his despair and his terrible guilt. He was sorry for almost everything he had done since he woke her up and he was, in the deepest part of himself, sorry for waking her at all.

He was sorry for building her.

He was sorry for conceiving her in his mind's eye.

He was sorry for thinking himself so wise and so capable.

So Edmond said nothing, to avoid saying everything.

Jeb came most often on Thursdays, late in the day as the sun was going down. Edmond wasn't sure that flying a helicopter at night was, strictly speaking, safe, but Jeb seemed comfortable with it. He touched down on a flat beach where the sand was beaten down from his repeated trips.

His load was particularly heavy this time and

Edmond was pressed into service along with Hart, helping to unload boxes and piling them neatly at the edge of the forest, far from the water.

"Be careful, ma'am," Jeb said to Hart. He always called her "ma'am," though he must have been a good twenty-five years her senior. "I've been hearing things about y'all. Looks like they may be coming down hard soon enough."

Hart smiled at him. Her smiles had become so rare and precious that Edmond paused, heavy wooden box in his arms, and simply looked at her.

"Thank you, Jeb. We are looking after ourselves," she said. She turned towards Edmond as though she had sensed his gaze. "We are looking after each other," she said.

Edmond was fairly certain that the army had not sanctioned the broadcast from an indie radio station. Breaking news about how high-level officials had pinpointed the likely location of rogue roboticist Edmond West and his "secret compound."

The wind, dull and buttery soft, moved through the half-crumbled walls of their little concrete home and Edmond could not help but quirk an eyebrow at the idea of a "compound." He felt certain that one needed at least four complete walls to make a compound.

Hart stood in front of these jagged, makeshift windows. Distantly, Edmond could make out the water, the strange occasional glint of starlight. He wondered if that was what she was looking at as well.

"We should go," Hart said. "The next favorable tide is at 4:37 a.m. We could have the boat ready by then. We can move further south. We haven't tried South America yet."

Edmond crossed the room to stand beside her. It was sort of beautiful, their trashed and abandoned little island. "Looks like rain to me," he said. There were indeed cast-iron clouds flitting occasionally across the moon. "I don't want to ride a boat in the rain, do you?"

Hart looked at him, incredulous. "But they're coming here."

Edmond just shrugged. "They are going to come to every place that we are, Hart. You know that."

Hart nodded. "I know that," she said.

"Sooner or later, they are going to come and we are going to be there," Edmond continued. "At least this time we know they're on their way."

Hart said nothing. In the silence, Edmond could hear the great crashing of the sea.

He could sense her uncertainty, it seemed as though she were vibrating with it.

He touched her arm, the skin he had made, tinted a shade he had selected, of a density he had calculated. "Hart. I'm tired."

She turned to him with a sigh that was only a little bit sad. "I know," she said.

"You don't have to stay with me," Edmond said, "I know you don't get tired."

"I have to stay with you," Hart said immediately. It was one of those rare moments when Edmond could see the machine in her, her cadence so stiff and immediate. It sounded like a lesson that had been beaten into her.

"We will wait together," she said, her manner softening. She took his hand and her own and moved towards the bed they had made, little more than a pile of linens and assorted soft items.

"Do you want to sleep?" Edmond murmured.

"No," Hart said.

She sat down on the bed, her hand still linked with his. Edmond stood before her but despite the height differential between them, he still felt somehow as though he were groveling to her. Begging for her forgiveness.

There was something so wise and so kind in her face.

"Can you forget what I am?" she asked him, softer than the sound of waves far behind them.

"Can you?" Edmond asked.

"You are Edmond," Hart said simply. "You are everything."

With his free hand, he touched her face and it seemed suddenly that he couldn't recognize any part of it. Had he mapped that nose? Built this eyebrow? In the half-dark, Hart was an entirely new creature. She came from nothing and from nowhere but instead sprung up from the earth like an ancient goddess.

Edmond kissed her and, for the first time, he knew what she tasted like. Her mouth was sweet and hot, like cinnamon. Her kisses were tentative but earnest and she made the smallest little sounds when they broke apart, as though she had surprised even herself.

Edmond pressed himself down on top of her and he could feel little earthquakes moving through her body. "I'm sorry," he found himself saying, "I'm so sorry. I'm so sorry for everything."

He said it again and again and Hart said nothing.

Her silence was not forgiveness, but it was not condemnation either.

Her hair covered them like a curtain and hid them from the sky above.

EPILOGUE

For the most part, Janelle did not concern herself with the search for Edmond West. Finding him was not her job and it wasn't a job she particularly wanted, at that. Still, even she could sense a kind of sea-change amongst those who had been consumed with the search.

It seemed there had been some kind of break and it looked like Edmond would be recaptured soon enough. At least, until someone leaked that information to the news media.

"Motherfuckers!" Liao shouted and it was audible all the way down the hallway. By the time he actually burst through the laboratory door, he was as angry as Janelle had ever seen him. "This is going to give him ample time to pack up and clear out." He was speaking to a younger man that Janelle didn't know, likely an assistant of some kind. "This is exactly what happened in Canada. The same exact thing!"

"Our people in the area indicate that they are still on the island and it doesn't seem like they are making any preparations to leave," the assistant offered, talking quickly as though it were an unpleasant task that he wanted to be done with as soon as possible.

Janelle cocked her head at the both of them, wondering why they couldn't have this conversation in, say, any other part of the building. She knew better than to say that, though, and instead just waited for Liao to address her.

"Captain Barber-Neal, we would like to use some Bots for this recovery mission."

"How many do you think you will need?" Janelle asked.

"How many are available?"

Janelle mentally flicked through the roster of Bots, all of those in the field or recovering from enhancement surgery or not yet finished with training. For months now, they had frozen the manufacture of new Bots, focusing solely on refurbishing the existing ones. "Roughly forty, sir."

General Liao nodded as though this number pleased him. "We don't have eyes on the island itself, so we have no real idea how many targets we are looking at. Theoretically, West could have dozens of his homemade Bots out there." He paused and knit his eyebrows. "Maybe that's why he isn't moving. He's spoiling for a fight."

"Edmond only has as many Bots as he can get materials for," Janelle said. She herself had consulted on an initiative to "starve out" Edmond by putting the squeeze on the global market in PolyX and nutrient solution and other things that he would need to develop more Bots. Of course, that program had only gone into effect after they started seeing Westian Bots out in circulation. There was no way of knowing exactly how many units Edmond had manufactured before then.

"I don't like ambiguities," General Liao said, almost as if he could hear her thoughts.

Janelle thought again about the limited Bot population languishing in the lab. In general, they tried not to keep too many Bots on base at any one time. After all, it had taken just one Hart Series to break Edmond West out. The only reason they had as many available units as they did was because of the concerted effort to round up defectors and install kill-switch technology. Many of the available Bots were in recovery after their operations.

"What exactly do you think you're going to need them for?" Janelle asked.

General Liao shook his head, annoyed. "Not sure. We're hoping that West will either be willing to sit for talks or can be captured relatively unaware."

"And you need more than forty Bots for that?"

"We are hopeful but not optimistic," Liao snapped.

It occurred to Janelle suddenly that she would almost certainly need to send Eb—HS C-27699. He had been essentially recovered for a week and a half now. Janelle had not yet given him his official sanction to go back to field work because she was, frankly, worried about his mental and emotional state.

He seemed to have curled in upon himself. He offered little information during any of his screenings and all other tests had indicated normal physiological and neurological reactions to stimuli. The staff nurses had urged Janelle to rubber stamp his paperwork, saying that he would work out any issues he might have on the job. But still Janelle resisted.

She would not be able to resist this.

"What happens if Edmond isn't willing to talk?" Janelle asked. It had not exactly surprised her when they started discovering fresh, non-military Bots in the wild. Edmond had chased his dream for most of his life, it wouldn't be at all like him to abruptly stop with all of his lofty goals unmet. But she couldn't imagine him returning to the fold. Try as she might, she couldn't picture him back in this lab, toiling away for their superiors.

"He's pumping unpredictable, dangerous advanced AIs onto the global stage," General Liao said, not without some compassion. It was worthwhile for Janelle to remember that Liao had hand-selected Edmond. He must have felt, then, as though he had plucked a diamond from a trash heap. "We cannot have that. We cannot. One way or another, we are going to dry up the stream of unsanctioned Bots."

One way or another.

Janelle wondered if she had always known that it would come to this. Perhaps not on that first day, when Edmond had appeared like an apparition, pale and thin and incapable of meeting her eyes. But it had not been long. There was something relentless in him and something . . . apocalyptic as well. He was going to change the world, he had said. And, sometimes, he had made her believe that.

Well, the world was changed now.

"I'll send you my Bots, if you promise to be careful with them," Janelle said finally.

General Liao looked affronted. "Of course," he said, "they're incredibly expensive."

—O—

All day, Janelle struggled with herself. Finally, fifteen minutes before she was set to head home, she exited the lab and made her way down to the medical quarters. HS C-27699 was in room 15, though the nurses were lobbying hard to have him moved to the barracks with the rest of the able-bodied Bots.

When Janelle came in, he was looking out the window at nothing in particular. His hair was coming back, about two inches of bristle-black stubble. He didn't turn around when she entered.

"HS C-27699," she said. It sounded, even to her, like an apology. "I just wanted . . . "

Janelle wasn't sure what she wanted.

She started again: "There's a big action coming up soon. You'll probably be involved."

By now, he had turned to look at her, but nothing in his face indicated any sort of recognition.

"And I just wanted to . . . to give you back your personal property."

She fished the fat little book out of her bag. It had gotten waterlogged at some point and, in the drying, had puffed up like an infected wound. Still, the text was readable and the cover was a vibrant, friendly blue. *20,001 Names for Your Bundle of Joy!*

She handed the book to C-27699 and he stared down at it grimly. He held it in both hands, compressing the swollen pages. His mouth worked uselessly. It suddenly seemed to Janelle that she was intruding on something very private. It nearly embarrassed her to look at him.

"I'll . . . I'll go . . ." Janelle said quietly, backing into the open doorway. He was still holding the book in front of him. He touched it like it was a holy text.

Janelle let the door swing shut behind her and walked briskly down the hallway. It was Friday. She would not return to the lab until Sunday afternoon. Likely, by then, Edmond West would have decided all of their fates. For now, she was going to go home and call her grandmother. She was going to make dinner. She was going to have a glass of wine before bed.

Janelle Barber-Neal was going to try her hardest to be human for a while.